ANY POSSIBLE OUTCOME

Any Possible Outcome

A Book of Urban Tales 2

K.C. TAYLOR

Sapati Ingera

CONTENTS

| 1 |

THE MEET UP

It was the last Monday before spring break. The sky was deep grey and the sound of the rain tapping on the windows declared a hushed mood throughout the building. The students at Carver Community School would have to make it to 3:45 on Friday before they could celebrate the two-week long hiatus of spring break. This was bittersweet news for Jazzlyn and her close friend Sierra. Like everyone else, they were excited to take a break from school, but they were upset about Sierra having to move to someplace in Florida.

The youngest of two girls, Jazzlyn was always busy. Her parents had her involved in many activities. Just to name a few, there was tumbling, piano lessons, soccer, and karate. She gave herself a nickname, AC- the activity kid. On the surface she was annoyed by all the activities, but deep down inside she enjoyed them.

Situated between a high school super athlete and a second-grade asthmatic action junky, Sierra was the opposite of Jazzlyn. She despised anything that would increase her heart rate. She indulged in books and puzzles for fun.

The halfway point of the day was celebrated by students and teachers alike on the middle school campus of Carver Community. Lunch was from noon until a quarter to one. Jazzlyn secured an open spot in the cafeteria, saved a seat for Sierra, then ransacked her paper bag lunch. After navigating the lunch line, Sierra joined Jazzlyn at the table. They sat in complete silence at first.

It was Jazzlyn who cut the tension. "Bro. Are you seriously about to leave me after this week?!"

"Yes, bro! But I don't want to." Sierra answered. She slammed her milk carton on the table.

"And how are you just gonna tell me about this last night?"

"My mama just told me yesterday! She didn't tell me sooner because she wanted to make sure we had a place to stay first."

"This is so messed up!"

"It is. But what's really messed up is that Kion gets to stay here."

"How did he get so lucky?"

"Baseball starts after break. He begged to stay to protect his senior status. Whatever that means."

It grew quiet again. Jazzlyn opened a bag of hot chips then brought up the conversation about how they first met. It was at a robotics competition when they were in the fifth grade. Their elementary schools squared off in the final battle.

Jazzlyn represented her school, the Golden Eagles and Sierra represented hers, the Commanders.

Their goal was to program their school's robot to lift plastic rings from the arena mat and navigate them to a holding box. Each team had been attempting to retrieve their last ring when their robots ran out of battery power at the same time. Both teams were declared winners that year. During the Carver Community orientation, the following school year, they recognized one another and became inseparable friends.

* * *

Jazzlyn navigated her after school routine like a pro. She blended in with the rest of the walkers after she helped Sierra chase down her little brother, Lamar, and carry him to the bus. Once she made it home, she flopped down on the beanbag chair in her bedroom. With an assortment of beats playing through her ear pods, she snacked on Goldfish crackers and sipped on a dark blue sports drink while dabbling with algebraic functions on her laptop.

At 5:02 Jazzlyn shut down the computer and opened her door just in time to hear her daddy yell, "Jazz! Get dressed! It's almost time to go!" She was already in her karate uniform and her belt was tied flawlessly. She used the extra few minutes to slump further down in the chair with her head lifted toward the ceiling. After listening to her fight song twice, she joined her dad in the car.

When she made it back home from karate practice, she took her Pitbull King, for a walk. He dragged her around their usual path, and he stopped to sprinkle on every vertical object along the way. Jazzlyn barged into her sister's bedroom and pretended to be interested in the makeup tutorial she was recording. Jazzlyn rearranged her products and made funny faces behind her back until she heard Nyla's expected cry, "Get out of my room!" She smiled to herself then went downstairs for another snack.

Jazzlyn rejected her daddy's offer to hit the boxing bag in the garage and politely declined her mama's invite to catch up on talk while dusting the books on the bookshelf. Instead, she made her way back upstairs to the loft. She got cozy in her game chair and turned the power on to the family's desktop computer. While waiting for it to boot up, Jazzlyn stared at the screen with wide eyes and great anticipation. Then like a trained diver perched on a springboard, she jumped in.

The online gaming environment was Jazzlyn's personal playground, and she became a different person in this vast habitat. She was known as hippitty hoppity or H2. Her code name offered the best description of her ability to multi-task. She would hop in and out of adventures while maintaining a high level of play in each game, and she could play at a steady pace for hours.

Jazzlyn sent and accepted invites from a host of friends in her gaming community, Sierra included. Sierra's code name was Kdub, short for krafty kid. Jazzlyn played and assisted in many adventures all during the evening, only pausing at her mama's demand to sit and eat dinner or lose computer privileges for three days. The last time she lost computer privileges set her back weeks in game play.

After an impressive three and a half hours of game play, Jazzlyn took off her headset and let out a mighty yawn. She staggered to her bed then swapped funny memes with Sierra. Jazzlyn fell asleep listening to her bedtime playlist.

* * *

The week before spring break was supposed to be slow, as most weeks before a break are. But in Jazzlyn's case, the days flashed by in a hurry. More of the same is the perfect cliché to describe how the rest of the week played out for Jazzlyn. The school vibe reeked of end-of-the-quarter exams, and after school, Jazzlyn continued to help Sierra capture Lamar and escort him to the bus.

At home she snacked on even more Goldfish crackers and sipped on more sports drinks. There was even more of the same from her karate sensei, "Jazzlyn, you're much too quiet." She made more sprinkle pitstops with King and triggered more rage from Nyla. Jazzlyn continued to reject at home PE class with her dad and her mama's requests to bond over all things super boring. And finally, there was more online gaming, the one constant that truly entertained Jazzlyn.

* * *

The two friends met up at their usual spot for lunch on Friday. They dined on Chik-Fil-A sandwiches and waffle fries. Sierra's mama had it delivered through Door Fast for the occasion of their last time eating lunch together. A few mutual friends wandered over to them to wish Sierra farewell. The food was delicious, but the tone was gloomy.

"Who am I supposed to hang out with now, bro?"

Sierra pointed to a table of four, where everyone was laughing hysterically. "How about with Whitney and crew?"

"Nah, they cool. But I like my eardrums."

"Agreed. Then how about with Julius and them?" They looked over in his direction. He sat at a table with four of his friends. All sat with their heads down and lost in their phones, not even looking up to put food in their mouths.

"No thanks. I do enjoy a little human interaction. Not much. But some."

"What about Xavier and Tanner?" They looked across the cafeteria to find Xavier standing on one leg in a yoga position while balancing a carton of milk on his nose. Tanner tossed craisins at his face hoping to get one in his mouth.

"Really?" Jazzlyn replied.

Sierra put her head down in shame. "Sorry."

"How about Kyla? She's in our online chat group."

"Yea. Maybe."

After lunch they went their separate ways. The afternoon classes were uneventful. After taking attendance, every teacher found the exact location of the movie they started the previous day after exams, then they pressed play. During last period, the students cleaned out their lockers. Jazzlyn was given permission to help Sierra return her books to the media center. That is when they confronted the reality of Sierra's departure and made a promise to always keep in touch.

Dismissal was a bit unusual. Sierra and Jazzlyn made an elaborate plan to trap Lamar before he had a chance to dash.

Instead, they found him standing next to the bus, motionless. Eye contact was made. But instead of running off, Lamar ran straight to Jazzlyn and put his arms around her. She hugged him back. Jazzlyn waited for Sierra and Lamar to be seated on the bus. She gave a final goodbye wave. As the bus pulled off, Sierra pulled the window down and yelled, "I'll text you later."

Friday evenings were Jazzlyn's favorite. She did not have homework, nor did she have any after-school activities. She took King for an extra-long walk around the neighborhood and then she flopped down next to Nyla on the sofa and watched their favorite GoTubers.

The moment her parents left the house for a date night, she tossed the remote to Nyla and took her place at the computer. She popped her knuckles, put on her headset, and entered the world of computer gaming, only pausing to check her phone for messages from Sierra. Jazzlyn's parents pulled into the driveway around 1:30 in the morning. She sent goodbye messages through the chat, ended all games, and shut down the computer. Jazzlyn disappeared into her bedroom before they opened the door.

***

Staycation. That is the word her mama used to describe the Stevenson's uneventful spring break. For the first time in years, there were zero plans to visit Florida. There were no reservations to stay at a big resort or fancy vacation home, nor were there any plans to visit grandma or feast on her home-made caramel cake. There were no day trips planned to one of the gazillion theme parks in central Florida. There was not even a plan for a beach day along the coast.

Spring break was at home on the west side of Indianapolis. Except for one rainy day, it was sunny and comfy the week before spring break with an average of 72. The first day of spring break, however, brought super chilly weather. It was damp and hovered near fifty degrees the entire week. It was a typical Indiana spring and Jazzlyn had no plans whatsoever. She spent the week off playing countless games on the computer. She only left the house to walk King or to attend karate practice.

She finally heard back from Sierra in the wee hours of the morning on the last Friday of the break. She was just about to sign off for the night when a message popped up on her screen. It was from kdub. It read, *guess who's back?!*

H2 quickly responded. *Yay where u been*

<Kdub>: *A long week and a longer story.*

<H2>: *Ur phone back on*

<Kdub>: *Nope. Another long story. But I'm getting a new one next week.*

<H2>: *Cool*

<Kdub>: *Chat again tomorrow?*

<H2>: *Yup @ 5*

<Kdub>: *Cool.*

<H2>: *later*

* * *

The Monday after break was like an expired bag of chips. There was no spice and no crunch. There was only yuckiness. Jazzlyn could hardly keep her eyes open, and it was the same way for many of the other students. She asked her third period teacher if she could skip lunch and slumber on the desk, but the teacher said no. Jazzlyn drifted to the cafeteria and found a spot at the quiet kid's table. She sat next to Kyla, and they shared strategies and game hacks.

Her afternoon classes were like an old bag of chips. There was a little spice and a tiny crunch. The vibe was not great, but doable. An hour of band took the sleepiness away, and she began to perk up a little more with each passing hour. Jazzlyn left with the first group of walkers at dismissal. She thought about Lamar and how much fun she and Sierra had getting him on the bus.

Jazzlyn took a long nap after karate practice. She jumped out of bed way past 9:00. Jazzlyn gorged down a plate of her mama's famous spaghetti then gulped down a glass of apple juice. She wrestled with King for a short while and then hid in her bedroom until the house grew quiet. Jazzlyn tiptoed into the loft at around 11:00 and turned on the computer. The gaming environment was like a fresh bag of chips. There was a zing and a crunch, and Jazzlyn was ready for both.

Jazzlyn logged on to the server of her new favorite game. Being the last survivor had become her obsession. It was the only game she had played since she beat a professional gamer in the final round of a tournament a few days earlier. As a result, he gave her a shout out on his GoTube page.

Sierra joined the server an hour later. They teamed up and dominated the dual's game. After several defeats they grew bored and started chatting.

\<H2\>: *yo*

\<Kdub\>: *yo*

\<H2\>: *im done*

\<Kdub\>: *so soon*

\<H2\>: *im bored*

\<Kdub\>: *u just need a challenge*

\<H2\>: *duh*

\<Kdub\>: *I got u*

\<H2\>: *what u mean*

Kdub\>: *click the link I sent. let me know what you think tomorrow*

\<H2\>: *cool*

\<Kdub\>: *later*

* * *

Aside from making it through the day at Carver Middle, Jazzlyn's focus was on the link Sierra had shared. It was a four-minute clip of a mobile gaming club known as The Meet Up. She could not stop thinking about the underground gamer's paradise. It teased her every waking moment. The spacious room was the size of a middle school gym. There was a soft green light seeping from the LED strips that outlined the perimeter from above. The background music matched the upbeat vibe and there was gaming action all over the place.

There were kids playing on consoles connected to huge TVs and PC kids, like herself, gaming on gigantic screens. There were kids playing on old school machines with joysticks, like the ones her dad once bragged about. One corner of the giant room was sectioned off for the VR kids. The video ended with a banner flashing across the screen. *Next stop- Indianapolis. Invitation only!*

Jazzlyn had not heard from Sierra, and she wanted so badly to talk to her about The Meet Up. She got her chance later that Thursday evening after her daily grind. Instead of turning in for the night, Jazzlyn waited until everyone else was asleep and opted in for extra gaming hours. Jazzlyn found the server Sierra was in and joined her. After teaming up and defeating countless opponents they started a chat session that lasted way past midnight. Jazzlyn waited for Sierra to bring up the video clip of the gaming club.

<Kdub>: so, what u think

<H2>: about what

<Kdub>: the meet up- duh

<H2>: it was cool

<Kdub>: that's all you have to say about it

<H2>: yup- kidding it was AWESOME

<Kdub>: guess what

<H2>: ???

<Kdub>: I got you an invite

<H2>: u did not

<Kdub>: yup I did

<H2>: but how

<Kdub>: Kion has a connect. I been bragging about your game play and he put in a word

<H2>: when is it

<Kdub>: tomorrow

<H2>: ???

* * *

Jazzlyn woke up the next morning in a daze, believing the conversation with Sierra and the invite to The Meet Up had never happened. She remembered one key detail that made her scramble to locate her phone for confirmation. The address to The Meet Up's secret location and time was saved as a note on her phone. As she got ready for school, she entertained the two dreams that resurfaced from the night before. They were both about her time at The Meet Up. In the first dream, she had become a legend in gaming after flexing her skills in front of several witnesses who quickly became fans. In the second dream, she played like a newbie and the name H2 was erased from the big book of gamers right in front of her, and then she was thrown out.

The school day went by in a blur. Jazzlyn kept to herself and did all that she was required to do while toying with the decision of whether to go to the Meet Up or not. On the walk home, she weighed the pros and cons of her dilemma. It was sixty-three degrees and sunny. She counted the good weather as a pro. She could make a name for herself in a bigger game community. Another pro. H2's popularity would jumpstart her career as a GoTuber and give her instant followers. Two more pros. She would have to find her own way to the secret location. That was the only con. By the time she made it to her front door, Jazzlyn decided that she was all in.

After eating her usual snack, Jazzlyn planked on her bed and listened to her playlist for comfort. She went over the information about the Meet Up and thought of a plan to get there and back without anyone finding out. The secret location was in the basement of a church around the corner from her former elementary school. The entry time was from 7:00-7:20. Sierra's brother Kion would be waiting for her inside the church.

Jazzlyn struck a deal with her sister. She agreed not to snitch on Nyla for having her boyfriend over. In exchange, Nyla would drive Jazzlyn to and from the elementary school. Jazzlyn convinced Nyla that she was meeting up with old friends for movie night at the school.

Jazzlyn thought about Sierra. She wanted to share the epic experience with her. She tried to find Sierra on their favorite game server, but it was too early to catch her. Jazzlyn logged into her School Connect account and typed her a brief message.

At 6:00 that evening Jazzlyn got permission from her dad to visit with friends from her old block. Nyla drove her to the school and parked outside the main entrance. The shades were pulled down on all the windows.

Nyla expressed her concern. "You sure about this Jazz? I don't see anybody."

"Yeah, I'm sure," Jazzlyn answered. "Thanks for the ride." She opened the door and rushed out of the car.

"If you say so. I'll wait here until you get in."

"No need! I forgot that I'm supposed to go to the back where the gym is. I'll text you when it's time to come get me. Bye! Love you!" Jazzlyn slammed the door shut.

Jazzlyn sprinted out of sight towards the back of the building. She peeked around the corner a minute later then exhaled when she saw Nyla's taillights fading in the distance. Jazzlyn looked at her phone and did some quick math. Only fifteen minutes had passed since she left home. Jazzlyn sat on a swing at the playground and allowed her mind to journey.

She went over the next few hours in her head the way a scene plays out on TV in slow motion. First, Jazzlyn would walk the four blocks to the church. After that she would dominate her favorite game in the company of her fellow gamers for an hour and fifteen minutes at the most. Then she would text Nyla to pick her up from the school. After that she would sprint back to the school just in time to get picked up by Nyla. They would make it home before their parents did. Finally, she would sit in her game chair, find Sierra, and tell her all about it. And so, it was settled. At 7:00 she would stop swinging, walk the four blocks to the church, and introduce H2 to the world.

WAIT! WHAT?!

"It's not supposed to be this hot! It's April!" Sierra complained. She was walking on the sidewalk with her mama on the way to the library.

"We ain't in the Midwest anymore, honey." Her mama answered. She opened the weather app on her phone. "But I feel you. Eighty-five degrees in April is just weird."

"Everything is weird."

"What do you mean?"

"Everything about this new place is weird, mama! The houses are spread far apart. There are swamps all over the place. The grocery stores and gas stations have strange names. Weird."

Her mama slowed her stride. "Look, I know you're not happy right now with being in a brand-new place. And I know how hard it is for you to be without a phone or Wi-Fi. But I had to do what's best for us. We'll get things popping again real soon."

"I hope so." They picked up the pace. "I hope the schools aren't weird too."

"You'll know soon enough," her mother teased. I'm printing off records today, and you and Lamar are back in desks come Monday!"

"Woo hoo," cried Sierra. "And let me guess. The mascot is an alligator."

They did not stop laughing until they walked into the library. The librarian stood behind an oval shaped desk in the center of the open room. As they approached the desk, Sierra let her eyes wander. It did not take long for her to notice the Teens Tech Lab in the southwest corner of the room. Flanked on both sides by all young adult books, was a display of large flat screen computers. She met eyes with her mother and was given the look of approval.

Sierra toured the bookshelves before settling in at a computer. She rubbed her hands together then logged on to her favorite gaming server. She instantly thought about Jazzlyn and how much fun they had gaming together. Sierra cracked a smile then switched over to her School Connect account.

She had to recall her username and all the weird characters that made up her password. When she finally got onto her message board, Sierra chuckled. Jazzlyn had messaged her first. Sierra opened the message and read it straight through. She moved closer to the screen and read it slower the second time. Sierra sprang up from the chair and cried, "Wait! What?!" She put her hand over her mouth and read the message one more time, out loud.

From the corner of her eye, Sierra's mother noticed her reaction. She excused herself from a conversation with the librarian and rushed toward Sierra. "What's the matter, Sierra?"

"I think Jazz might be in trouble, mama!"

"What are you talking about?"

"Read this message." Sierra stepped out of the way. Her mama stood in front of the computer and read the message out loud.

Sup Sierra,

Thanks for the invite to the meet up. You prob think I wasn't going but I am.

I'll be leaving out soon, in fact. Wish you were here to go with me. Hanging out in the basement of a church in the old hood is kinda sus. TG Kion will be there.

I'll know at least one face. I'll tell you all about it later.

After she read it, she looked at Sierra with confusion on her face. "I don't get it, honey. How is Jazz in trouble?"

"Mama! I haven't spoken to Jazz since we left Indy. That invite didn't come from me."

"Oh." Her mother took a moment to think about it. "Oh!" She repeated. "Oh no! When did she send it?"

"About thirty minutes ago!"

"We have to stop her!" Sierra's mama took her phone out of her purse and gave it to Sierra. "Take this outside and call Jazz!"

"But I don't know her number by heart!"

"Then call Kion! Get him to go over there and stop her!"

Jazzlyn ran outside with her mama's phone. She called her brother, Kion, but he did not answer. Sierra kept calling until he finally did. She fumbled the message at first, but once Sierra put the words together, Kion accused her of playing a prank and ended the call.

Sierra's mama took the phone from her and called Kion back. She told him about Jazzlyn's message and the urgency of the situation. "Now get to that girl's house right now and warn her and her parents!"

"Yes ma'am! I'm grabbing my hoodie and I'm leaving now."

* * *

Nyla answered the door after she stopped King from barking. Kion took a deep breath then asked if he could come in. Nyla recognized him from the basketball team, and she knew that he was Sierra's brother. Still, she was suspicious of him, so she called out to her boyfriend, Chris, who was hiding in the coat closet. "You can come out, Chris. False alarm. It's not my folks."

Chris stepped out and stood by Nyla as she invited Kion in.

Kion cleared his throat. "Is Jazz here? I got a message for her."

"No."

"Is your mama and daddy here?" His voice was deep and shaky.

Nyla looked at Chris and then back at Kion. "I think you already know the answer to that."

"Look. I was sent over here by my mama and sister to give Jazz and your parents a message."

"Well, it's date night for the parents, and Jazz is at a school function. You'll have to tell me instead."

Kion relayed the warning about the trouble Jazzlyn was in. He looked at Nyla then blurted out, "I'll drive if you want me to!" Nyla grabbed the house key and all three bolted out the door. Kion led the footrace to his car.

BAD INTENTIONS

Tommy and Duck made it to the church an hour before Jazzlyn did. The sun had just been tucked in and the evening sky was a shade darker than grey. Tommy parked the unmarked van in front of an abandoned house, reclined in the driver's seat, then took a lengthy pull from an e-cig. His wrinkled face was pale and dirty and littered with untamed whiskers. Tommy had worked in the IT department of a computer store for many years, until he was fired for masterminding a heist on his day off. After a six-year prison sentence he joined an underground crime network as a seeker and transporter.

Tommy turned off the police scanner then gave Duck a verbal orientation. Duck was Tommy's neighbor and new apprentice. He was young, black, and handsome with an athletic frame. Duck's speed and agility made him the perfect recruit for Tommy's transport missions.

"Each job requires a three-step process," explained Tommy.

He told Duck that the first step in the process was the set-up. It was the most difficult and involved a lot of hacking. It required Tommy to learn the unique online habits of an unsuspecting teenager.

"You won't have to worry about step one at all." Tommy took another pull from his e-cig then smiled. "The set-up is all mine."

Tommy described the second step, receiving the package. It consisted of a simple yet calculated snatch-and-grab, followed by a vehicle transfer and then a road trip to a drop off location.

"This second step, Duck, is where you earn your pay." Duck nodded in agreement.

Tommy labeled the final step, the drop-off, as the riskiest. It involved driving to an unknown destination in which the location would be sent through text every half hour along the route. The most dangerous part about the drop-off, he explained, would be the negotiations. They would have to surrender their phones and guns and meet face-to-face with a hostile boss surrounded by stocky bodyguards holding semi-automatic weapons.

"It's a tough job," said Tommy. "But trust me when I say the cash reward is worth every second of it."

Their conversation dwindled after talking about the three-step-process. Duck asked a few random questions, but it was mostly quiet in the van. Tommy glanced at the time then reset his seat to an upright position. He examined their surroundings through every window then squinted at Duck, "Where's your skully?"

"Right here."

"Blindfolds?"

"Check."

Tommy grabbed his skull cap and gloves from the backseat. When he turned back around, he looked through the rearview mirror and saw a thin figure speedwalking up the sidewalk. It was Jazzlyn. Tommy looked over at Duck. "Do you see her?"

"Yup. And she's coming right this way. Too easy."

"Let's wait until she passes. Then you're gonna grab her in front of the church."

"Just give me the word."

"You ready for this, Duck?"

"I was born that way."

"Alright then. Let get these coins."

* * *

"Please drive faster, Kion!" Nyla yelled from the passenger's seat.

"I'm going as fast as I can!" He responded. "I'm even running through red lights!"

"I feel horrible," Nyla cried. "I knew something was up! The school looked closed. And she was trying to rush me!"

"It's not your fault," Chris tried to reason with her from the back seat. He rubbed her neck and shoulders. "You didn't know. But don't worry, we'll get to Jazz in time. Right Kion?"

"Yeah!" Kion choked the stirring wheel as he remembered that his name was involved in the imposter's plan to trick Jazzlyn. Kion peeked at Nyla, "Don't worry. We're gonna save her."

They made it to the neighborhood in eight minutes. Their eyes scanned every street and alleyway. Kion decreased his speed once he arrived at the school. There was no sign of activity, and the parking lot was empty. Even the night custodian's car was gone. From the school, he drove west to the closest church in the neighborhood.

Chris bolted out the car when Kion came to a complete stop at the church. He checked the main doors, but they were locked. He ran around the building and got in through the back door. Chris followed the sound of voices to the main sanctuary and barged in. All conversations ceased and everybody froze. The whole choir watched in silence as Chris gazed around. After a few awkward moments, the choir director ordered Chris to leave. He returned to the car without any news.

Kion drove in the direction of the other church. As soon as he turned the corner, Nyla yelled out, "Look! There she is!" She pointed Jazzlyn out to Kion and Chris.

As Kion was closing in on Jazzlyn, they saw two men emerge from a white van. Jazzlyn was unaware of it, but Duck was right behind her, following closely. Tommy stood outside the van. Kion put all his weight down on the gas pedal and raced ahead.

Jazzlyn felt a tug on her shoulder. She spun around, grabbed Duck's wrist, and gave him a butterfly kick to the knee. Duck's leg buckled but he did not fall until Jazzlyn spun around again and kicked him in his privates.

Kion pulled up at that exact moment. He flicked on the high-beam lights and slammed on the brakes. Nyla had her hand pressed against the horn the whole time. Tommy ran to Duck and helped him off the ground. They turned away quickly and ran back to the van. Tommy started the van then sped off.

Nyla, Kion, and Chris got out the car and ran to Jazzlyn. She was shaking uncontrollably and sobbing. Nyla put her arms around her little sister and squeezed her tightly. Chris snapped a few photos of the van as it fled the scene, and Kion dialed 911.

TWO WEEKS LATER

Jazzlyn's parents were in constant contact with the authorities. The police issued an APB for the white van, conducted a lengthy interview with Jazzlyn, and reported the incident to the F.B.I. After hearing back from the F.B.I., the police told the Stevenson's that the two men who tried to kidnap Jazzlyn, were likely part of a human-trafficking ring. The investigation slowed at that point due to several key factors. First, there was no physical description of Tommy and Duck. Secondly, the van did not have a license plate to trace. And lastly, Tommy left no digital footprint.

Jazzlyn was a different person after that crazy night. She had aged by at least five years. She was pleased with her home-based gaming sessions even though the number of minutes she spent on the computer was drastically decreased and severely monitored. Sierra started her new school in Florida, and she finally got a new phone. Jazzlyn and Sierra agreed to conversate over the phone before meeting up online.

THE END

| 2 |

MIND TRAP

October 14, 2024

I can't decide yet. Is my new life a good thing or a bad thing? I'm getting more sleep now. That's a good thing. I'm not quite sure of what's ahead for me. Do I continue to look over my shoulder, or do I finally relax? This uncertainty is a bad thing.

I'm in the rambling stage. This is according to my new friend Breanna. I met Bre a few weeks back, not too long after I made it to town. I've never been to a therapist before, but I imagine it to be a lot like spending time with Bre. We would be in the middle of a long conversation before I suddenly realize that I'm expressing my deepest feelings to her. Again. I find myself spilling all types of details about things that happened to me in my past. Bre is super clever, and she is a good listener.

I could have called her nosy and dismissed her early on. But the truth is, I like her. And I like telling her about my life and the things that I ran from. Especially since I'm practically all alone here. But it's not just all about me, we talk about all types of things.

In order to get out of this rambling phase, I must reflect on the events of the last few months. And then I must let them go. Every last one of them. This is all according to Bre of course, but I think she may be on to something.

What if I did take a pause to actually reflect? I might be able to discover a clear path to my future. And at the very least, I might get my appetite back and shake this feeling of being stuck. Besides, the time is right for a reflection over my entire life and not just the craziness of the last three months. So, I guess I'll give this reflection thing a try. And if my instincts are right, I'll no longer be trapped.

Until next time,

JBJ

THE EARLY YEARS

My name is Robert Cisneros, but I go by Rob or JBJ depending on the person talking to me. I'm sixteen years old, and I'm mixed with Black and Puerto Rican. I am the only son of Sharice Cisneros and Juan Cisneros, also known as Juice Berry or JB. My dad is Puerto Rican and well known in the old neighborhood back in Indiana. He was sent to Lakeside Correctional Facility when he was about my age. He was sentenced to 15 years but served 10 on account of good behavior. He practically grew up in prison.

He served his time but found it impossible to find work when he got out. He kept searching until one day he found a factory job across the bridge in Chicago. He made the daily commute on the south shore train from East Chicago, Indiana to Chicago, Illinois. He did this until he saved up enough money to leave my grandma's house. Once he did, he settled into an old apartment down the street from his job.

The company he worked for hired formerly incarcerated men and paid them well. The owners bought an old building and turned it into a workout gym for their employees. It was nicely equipped with weights, workout benches, a track, and a full-size basketball court. My dad still brags about how good that job was.

My parents were a couple before my dad went to prison. My mama took him back when he got out, but only after waiting to see how he would adjust to life outside the concrete walls. She moved into the apartment with him and found a job waiting tables at a fancy restaurant downtown in the loop. I was born in that small apartment a year after my mama joined my dad in Chicago. I don't have any memories about it because we were forced to leave and move in with my grandma after my dad's good factory job quickly packed up and left the Midwest.

I was six months old when my parents moved back across the state line to East Chicago, Indiana. They tell me that my grandma was overjoyed to have us at home with her, but she passed away soon after we moved in. I don't remember her, but my parents told me many stories about her that match well with the dozens of pictures she took with me when she was still alive.

On top of planning a funeral and caring for an infant, my parents struggled to find work and keep food on the table. My dad's cousin, Big Mike, who he served time with, helped with the funeral costs and with putting food on the table. He said it was the least he could do for his favorite auntie.

After a few bad months, my mama found a job at a daycare center and my dad returned to the job of his youth, working on cars with his uncle Chad. Uncle Chad closed his make-do shop a few years earlier, but my dad was desperate to make a living, so he convinced him to reopen it.

Things started looking a lot better after my first few years of life. My parents got married at the county building when I was three. My mother held on to her job and took over as manager for the owners when they retired. My dad persuaded Uncle Chad to expand the shop.

Big Mike stepped in again to help with the renovation, but my dad made it clear that he was to have no part in the business itself. The make-do shop became an official car shop, and my dad and uncle named it Chad's Car Care.

I spent my toddler years at the daycare with my mama. When I became old enough to start kindergarten, my mama enrolled me in a traditional school. When school was over, I mostly spent time laughing and playing with my cousin Co-Co under the careful watch of my mama's sister, Aunt Kim. My childhood years were happy and carefree.

TRAGEDY

By the time I made it to middle school, everything started to change, and I'm not just talking about my body either. I grew stronger and taller physically, but my growth was stunted emotionally when my mama suddenly died from cancer. She was there one day, and things were good and normal, then she was gone the next day, and nothing made sense anymore.

After she died, I stopped going to school. Nobody noticed or cared. I spent my days sleeping in and wandering along the railroad tracks behind the house. I would lay down on the cold metal tracks until I heard the sound of the warning signal in the distance. Then I would press my ear to the track until it started to tickle from the vibration. That was my cue to stand up and take five giant steps back and wait for the train to speed past me with incredible sound and power.

My mom's death shook my dad too. He picked up extra hours at the shop and stumbled in the house late at night, sometimes with two empty liquor bottles still clutched in his hands. He would yell at me to go to bed before passing out on the couch. We were both lost.

Things continued like this for a few months until the day my dad put an end to it. I left the house one afternoon to go to my spot along the railroad tracks only to find him already there. I sat down beside him on and old crate and he put his arm around me.

He told me the story of how he fell apart after my grandma passed away. He told me that things went really dark for him, and that my mama almost left him because of it.

"What made her stay?" I asked him.

"I changed."

"How did you find the strength?"

"It was something your mama said. She told me that life and death were one in the same. She said that everyone who lives will certainly die and that includes the people we love the most. She said that we honor our loved ones in their death by living our best lives."

My dad quietly wept, and so did I.

I heard the train's signal in the distance and urged my dad to complete the ritual with me. We must have looked like drugged out zombies with our ears pressed to the train tracks, but I didn't care. When I felt the vibration, I asked my dad if he felt the same thing. He did. I told him to stand up. We took five giant steps back then watched in awe as the train flashed by. He didn't say so, but I could tell he felt the same thing I felt. He looked at me and told me to never do that again. And I never did. I didn't need to.

THE CREW

Uncle Chad skipped town without a word. I guess my mom's death really did a number on him too. Uncle Chad left the shop to my dad, and my dad added some new services and picked up a few more loyal customers. He even hired two new people and put them on full time.

I settled back into school and leaned heavily on my crew. First up is my homeboy, Dwayne. We call him Dewy because he's always freestyling. He said his flow is cold and nice like Mt. Dew. Unlike the rest of us in the crew, Dewy is a true athlete and lives on the basketball court. He plays for the school and he's in several other leagues. I've known Dewy since elementary school.

Tony Junior is my other homeboy. We just call him Junior. His dad and my dad are best friends. They were the two youngest of their crew back in the day. Junior is the one with the hot temper and the street ambitions.

Then there is my cousin Corwin, the youngest in the crew. We call him Co-Co. We've always had each other's back ever since we were little. If one of us got in trouble the other one did too. Co-Co faithfully checked-in on me after my mama died, and I was there for him last March, when he really needed me.

It happened over a year ago, a week after we both turned fifteen. We were born two days apart. I had been calling and texting Co-Co, but he was ghosting me. After watching Dewy play in tournament game at the park, I decided to drop in on him. I knocked on the door, but nobody answered, so I let myself in.

The house had changed since my Aunt Kim moved to Atlanta, but not in a good way. I didn't see Uncle Jeff's car outside, so I yelled out to Co-Co, and he answered from the back of the house. I walked in his bedroom then I froze. He held a pistol to the side of his temple.

Once we made eye contact, he rested the gun in his lap and told me I was just in time. I sat next to him on the floor, and I pleaded with him not to do it. He said that I didn't understand. I told Co-Co that I did understand. I knew for a long time that my cousin was gay. I knew that he struggled with coming out because he never did. I didn't know that it bothered him to the point of wanting to kill himself.

I couldn't exactly relate to what he was going through, but I felt his pain. As he sat there, caressing the gun like a pet, he told me that he'd came out to his dad earlier that morning. I couldn't hide the look on my face because I knew what was coming. Dads like ours, who grew up in the nineties, have a hard time accepting that two people of the same sex can have love for one another.

But I was wrong. He said that his dad stopped him in mid-sentence and told him that he already knew, and that he accepted him for who he was. I told him that was the best possible outcome.

I stared at him for a few seconds before I asked, "What's up with the gun, cuz?"

"It was something he said, Rob."

He told me that after his dad gave him his support that he hugged him and warned him to be careful when he came out to the rest of the family and the people in the neighborhood.

"I thought telling my dad would be the hardest part. But it's not."

I casually took the gun from him. I removed the clip, cleared the chamber, and then tossed it on the bed.

"Everybody already knows that you're gay, cuz."

"What?"

"It's true. How do you think you got the name Co-Co?"

After a really good laugh I told him to stop trippin'. I reminded him of who he was and told him that everything would work out and that he didn't have to rush anything. He thanked me, and then I gave him a hug. He slipped out of my grip, put me in a headlock, and told me not to tell anymore gay jokes. I agreed.

THE OFFER

My house had always been the official handout spot for the crew. We were kickin' it there one evening when I got an unexpected visit from my dad's cousin, Big Mike. He hung out with us for a while playing video games and telling us stories from back in his day. After a bit he told the crew that he wanted to speak to me alone.

By the way, it was Big Mike who gave me the name JBJ, which stands for Juice Berry Junior. He said I had the same swag my dad once had. Co-Co called me Rob, but the rest of the crew also called me JBJ, but not in front of my dad. According to him, that name holds too many bad memories.

Dewy, Junior, and Co-Co started hanging out on the front porch and left us to talk. Big Mike cleared his throat before telling me his version of how he and my dad got locked up back in the day. He took the blame for everything that went down and promised to repay him for all that time he lost. He told me that part of his plan to pay it back, was to look out for me.

I knew what he was up to. Everybody knew what was going to happen when Big Mike got home from prison. He was on the way up before he went in, and now he's on top. If it was illegal and sold anywhere in East Chicago, it came through Big Mike. I didn't want anything to do with what Big Mike was about to say to me, but I wasn't about to be disrespectful, so I heard him out.

I was right. Big Mike offered me some work that he described as safe and profitable. He stood up to leave and pulled a lump of cash out of his pocket. He counted and separated out five Benjamin's and put them in my hand.

"Happy belated birthday, JBJ."

When he left the crew came back in. I turned the music back up while Junior and Co-Co turned back on the game system and continued their battle. Dewy started texting back and forth with his girlfriend, and he eventually convinced her to come through with some of her friends.

My dad walked in from the shop a few hours later. That is when we shut things down. I said bye to the crew and retired to my room for the night.

THE CLOSE IN

A few months went by before I saw Big Mike again. To keep it real, I was ghosting him. I didn't want anything to do with him or his activities. Now that I think about it, my crew was avoiding me like I was avoiding Big Mike. Co-Co was the only one I heard from, but I wasn't bothered. I was too busy joyriding in my new ride, a candy apple red cobalt with sweet custom wheels. It wasn't exactly new, but it was all mine and it whipped well.

My dad surprised me with it. He told me that he was proud of me for all the work I was putting in at the shop. But I think it was his way of keeping me away from the lure of the street hustle.

I was out riding with Co-Co one Saturday afternoon, when I ran into Big Mike. I spotted his parked car in front of the gas station when I pulled up to the pump. He wasn't in his car, so I figured him to be inside the station chatting it up with the attendant. I used my dad's debit card to put $10 in the tank, and then I tried to make a quick exit. But the second I opened the door to get in, Big Mike walked out and yelled out to me, "Ay, JBJ!"

I walked up to him, "What up big cuz!"

"What's up lil' cuzzo? I haven't heard back from you."

We shook up. Then I responded, "I know, man. That's my bad."

He told me to get in my car and follow him. Now, I could have just left and went about my business, but I had to be smart. I didn't need the trouble of getting on his bad side, so I did what I was told.

I followed him to one of his houses in the harbor. There were two cars parked in front. Me and Co-Co followed him inside. Junior, Dewy, and a couple other people I knew where there sitting around as if they had been waiting on Big Mike to return. Suddenly it made sense why I hadn't heard from my crew.

Big Mike told us to sit down then he turned off the TV. He got straight to the point. "Look around, y'all. This here is the winning squad. JBJ, I'm putting you with Junior. Co-Co, you're ridin' with Tim. And Dewy, you're with Bunk."

I couldn't believe what I was hearing. He was calling plays like an NBA coach.

"Each driver now has a spotter," he continued. "Other than that, everything else is the same. Just like we practiced. Stick to the plan and do not deviate!"

"And what exactly is the plan?" I demanded to know. "I don't remember that part."

Big Mike laughed a little, "Relax JBJ. You ask too many questions. I told you I got you. Easiest job ever."

"Ain't this some shit." I said that to myself, but the anger inside of me was starting to boil over. I couldn't believe what was happening. Something told me to hold my tongue, and it was probably a good thing that I did.

Big Mike gave an order for me, Co-Co, and Dewy to text him once the drop was made. After that, he was gone. I waited until his car left the driveway, and then I got up to leave. Junior gave me a shove and asked, "Where you going?"

"You can't be serious right now! Junior, if you put your hands on me again, we're fightin' till the death!"

He backed up. I turned my untamed anger towards Co-Co. "Are you leaving or are you with these fools?"

I dropped Co-Co off at his crib and drove straight home. The joy was all gone from my riding on account of the stunt Big Mike tried to pull. He straight tried to usher me right into his criminal enterprise, and he tried to do it without my consent. I knew that I was going to have to answer for walking out on a job, but so be it. I was determined to stand firm whenever that moment came.

A confrontation came moments later when I arrived home. But it wasn't with Big Mike, it was with my dad. I walked into the house and found him sitting alone at the kitchen table. It was definitely unusual because the TV was off and so were all the lights except the old and dinky lamp that was oddly placed on the kitchen table. I figured he had something heavy on his mind, so my intention was to tiptoe through the kitchen and settle in my room without being noticed. But he did notice me, and he told me to sit down.

I sat down across from him in a chair that was intentionally placed there. "What's up, pops? Everything ok?"

"I think you know what's up, Rob. We could sit here for hours playin' games or we could get down to business and have ourselves an honest conversation."

I was tired and not in the mood for whatever was happening. But still I responded, "I choose b. What's the topic of our conversation?"

"Big Mike got you sellin' drugs for him!?"

"What!? No!"

"Don't you sit here and lie to me, Rob! I see the new clothes and stuff! And I saw you parked outside his house earlier!"

I couldn't believe what I was hearing. My anger shot up to one hundred. My mama's spirit must have held me down because even though my anger spiked, it simmered away and turned into a deep compassion for the concern that my dad had for me.

I took a deep breath and then started to explain. I told him that I bought a pair of J's and some new drip with the birthday money Big Mike had given me. Then I told him that me and the crew hung out for a bit at Big Mike's house. I knew there were old wounds between my dad and his cousin, so that's all that I told him.

I looked him in his eyes, "You don't ever have to worry about me working for Big Mike."

We sat in silence for a few minutes. Then my dad started cracking up. He stopped laughing long enough to tell me the story about how Uncle Chad questioned him about working for Big Mike. My dad was the same age as me when this happened. Uncle Chad turned his office into an interrogation room and confronted my dad while sitting in a backwards chair with a Newport in his mouth.

My dad chuckled some more then looked at me. "I'm no Uncle Chad. But how did I do?"

I looked around at the weird setup, "Nah!" We cried tears of laughter that night.

I stayed in my room most of the next day. The rain was heavy, and my mood was sleepy. I stayed in bed well past 11:00. I woke up at 10:00, but I entertained the thoughts in my head before I actually got up. I considered Big Mike's proposal. Then I thought about Dewy and Junior and how eager they were to be put on. I also thought about my dad and how he wanted to protect me from the mistakes he made when he ran with Big Mike. I wondered if I would have made the same mistakes back then. I would have been smarter.

My thoughts were interrupted by a knock at the door. My dad left for work earlier that morning to get caught up on paperwork, so I had no choice but to answer. I was caught off guard when Big Mike pushed through the door and let himself in.

He walked past me and headed straight to the living room. I closed the door and followed behind him, ready to throw hands if it came to that. But it didn't. He wasn't even upset. He lit up a blunt then started spilling some smooth talk.

"Don't even worry about yesterday, JBJ," he started. "You weren't ready, and I don't blame you." He waited for my reply.

"You're right. I wasn't. And I'm never gonna be ready. That ain't me."

"Oh, it's you alright. You're a Cisneros ain't you?"

"Look, Big Cuz, I appreciate the offer, but that ain't me. And you gotta bounce."

He laughed at me. "Alright, JBJ. I'm about to leave. And I'm gonna be real patient with you, baby cuz. You know where to find me when you come to your senses. And I know where to find you."

I slammed the door after he left, angered by his arrogance. He was trying to back me into a corner, and I developed a hate for him. I went back to my room and started doing pushups. I lost count of how many sets of twenty I did. I kept going until my arms turned into noodles, and I could no longer lift myself up.

THE DECISION

I was determined to not fall in line with Big Mike. I kept a busy weekday routine by going to school and putting in a few hours at the shop. While managing this routine, I constantly thought about something Co-Co suggested a while back.

After Big Mike's last ambush, I texted Co-Co to tell him what was said. He texted back and said that Big Mike had just left his house talking the same smooth talk. We laughed at his rehearsed speech. He said that he was not mad at us for walking out on a job. Then he promised to wait for us with open arms and treasures untold, when we finally decided to join him.

Co-Co's next message read, "*We should leave this place and start over in Atlanta.*" I stared at the screen. It caught me off guard because I was not ready to fully consider a move. I simply responded by texting, "*Maybe.*"

As days turned into weeks, I started to reconsider what a fresh start in a new place would look like. I was doing my best at school, but I came to the realization that school was just a mandatory institution with little value. When I did go, I completed the work I was assigned, but I was not challenged or inspired. It was a waste of my time.

It was pretty chill working with my dad and the other old heads at the shop. The work was easy enough. I was an expert at changing oil, and I organized everything from receipts to lug nuts. I stayed laughing at the strange advice they gave me when I got into arguments with my girlfriend, Kenzie. Their *when I was your age* stories were hilarious too. Working at the shop kept gas in my tank and it allowed me to save a few pennies, but there was no future there for me.

Me, Kenzie, and Co-Co hung out at the bowling alley on weekends. A lot of our friends from school did the same. We didn't go there to bowl. We went there to lounge in the cafe, feast on nachos, and gulp down jarittos.

I'll never forget the last time we hung out there. It was on a Saturday evening. I was the last one to arrive. I made a pitstop at the house for a shower and some clean clothes after working all afternoon in the shop. We must have been feeling adventurous that night. I can't remember whose idea it was to actually bowl, but it was Kenzie and me against Co-Co and his friend Kevin from Merriville. We made it through all the shenanigans and managed to finish the game. Kenzie and I won with a combined score of 140, 90 of them was hers.

We found a table in the cafe and settled down. Junior and Dewy walked in at some point during the evening. Dewy was naturally flashy, but now my guy Junior was too. He no longer had to wear hand me downs from his older brothers. Junior's fit and shoe game had a major upgrade, and he acquired a nice jewelry collection. I was happy for my guy, in a tense sort of way.

I yelled out to them and invited them to our booth. We pulled two tables together to make enough room for them and the girls in their company. We shared junk food, we drank jarittos, and we laughed. We mostly cracked up at Dewy's random freestyles. The crew was back together again.

Kevin left the table to order a pizza. Junior also left to take a private call. Dewy took Junior's spot, leaving the girls together at their own table. With a straight face, Dewy asked what we were waiting on. He practically scolded me and Co-Co for not joining with him and Junior to work for Big Mike.

"Look, man. That just ain't me." I told him.

"Makin' a lot of money ain't you?" He teased.

"I'm happy for y'all, but I'm not tryin' to get caught up like my pops did."

"Big Mike was right. Your dad's downfall got you shook."

"Be careful, Dewy. And I'm not shook."

"Look around, JBJ. What's your plan? What's the future lookin' like for you?"

His intentions were good, but I was starting to get annoyed. "I'll be alright, Dewy. Now change the subject!"

"Bet. Let's change the subject. But one last thing, and then I'm done. Things are much different. Your big cousin is the man. He hosts fancy dinners with a team of lawyers and businessmen every week. Let that sink in."

Just then, Junior came back to the table, but he didn't sit down. He looked at Dewy and said, "We gotta bounce!" Dewy stood up and they both took off toward the nearest exit. I didn't care about their speedy departure. I sat there with a half-smile on my face. I was happy to be uninvolved.

Junior and Dewy left without saying a word to anybody. They didn't even say goodbye to their dates, Tiny and Liz. It was awkward for a minute, until Kevin showed up with a deep-dish pepperoni pizza. We all squeezed into the same table. Co-Co turned up the volume to the song he was listening to and we got it poppin' again.

Things started to wind down after 11:00. Co-Co rode with Kevin to take Tiny and Liz home. Me and Kenzie stayed cozy at the table until it was closing time. As we were walking toward the exit, Kenzie turned toward me and pulled me in for a hug.

She lifted up on her tiptoes and whispered in my ear, "I gotta tell you something."

"Oh, shit!" I'm not ready to be a daddy.

"Not that." She read my thoughts.

"Okay, good. Then what is it?"

"I'm leaving East Chicago." There was a long pause. "My family is moving to Indianapolis."

"When?"

"Tomorrow."

I didn't know how to respond. I wanted to be angry or sad, but I didn't feel either way. I understood why people left the region when opportunity showed up. In my head, I was applauding her parents.

I pulled her in for a long hug. "You should have told me sooner." We held each other for a while and then we started walking again. The spring winds that blew in from Lake Michigan made it a cold night. We raced to my car. I unlocked the door for Kenzie then I went to the back seat to grab my jacket for her.

There was something strange under my jacket. I stopped and stared at it for a moment. Then I started to doubt was it actually was. It was the size of a brick, and it was heavily wrapped in plastic. Someone put a block of drugs in the backseat of my car.

I snatched the jacket and slammed the door. I pulled Kenzie out of the front seat, then gave her the jacket to put on.

"I caught a flat! Let's walk to the burger joint. I'll call us a ride from there."

It was too cold for me and Kenzie to hold a conversation as we walked, but it was just right for me to think things through. There were a few details to the mystery of the brick, that had to be more than just a coincidence.

First there was Junior. He was texting a lot when he first got to the bowling alley, and then he left to take a call. When he came back, he set my keys on the table and said that I dropped them. After that, him and Dewy bounced. A few minutes later a guy who was obviously a cop dressed in street clothes walked into the bowling alley. He was searching for somebody. An hour after that is when I got a text that read, "You know what to do." I paid it no attention. I knew that whoever sent it, was texting the wrong person.

We cuddled in a booth at the White Castle. Neither of us had much to say. She was probably focused on the move to Indianapolis and my thoughts were on how to get the brick out of my car. When Kenzie's brother came to pick her up, we shared a long embrace and then I watched her leave.

My dad showed up a few minutes later. He pulled up in his utility truck, ready to tow my car to the shop. The plan was to leave it there overnight so that he could work on it in the morning. We were a block away from the bowling alley when I told my dad to not to stop. I told him about the breakup and that I was tired, annoyed, and wanted to go home.

"Alright, Rob. But you sure about leaving your car there?" He asked.

"I'm sure."

"Alright then," he replied. "We'll swoop by and pick it up in the morning."

I leaned against the door and closed my eyes. I thought about all types of ways to handle the problem. *Do I reach out to him? Probably not. I would be coming in way too hot. Do I wait for him to reach out to me? Hell no! His arrogant ass would want me to move the brick. Do I let my dad in and see what strategy he would come up with? Nope. His distrust of his cousin would turn into violence and send him back to prison.*

We made it home that night in no time. I rejected my dad's offer to talk about the breakup, and I ignored the repeated calls from Kenzie. The closure had already happened, and there was no reason to drag it on. I had just finished a second set of pushups when Big Mike called.

"What up!?"

"What's up JBJ? I hear you sittin' on something that belongs to me. Why haven't you brought it to me yet?"

"We've been over this Big Cuz. I don't work for you."

"And that's too bad. Because if you did work for me, I wouldn't have to worry about you hanging out with your friends in the middle of a job."

"That's tough."

"Look JBJ, It's not your mess up. But I need you to bring it to me tonight. Like right now."

"There're two things wrong with that. I don't work for you and I don't have it."

"What do you mean you don't have it?!"

"It's still in my car at the bowling alley. And I don't plan on ever touching it!"

"If my brick ain't where you say it is, that's strike three!"

He hung up and I continued to do my pushups. It's not a good thing to be young and feel closed in. School wasn't working, there was no desired future for me at the shop, and there was a big bully after my soul. I called Co-Co and asked him if he still wanted to move to Atlanta. I told him I was ready.

MOVING DAY

Moving day was months ago. It was the middle of July and hotter than the devil's breath. I was able to stuff my personal belongings into an old duffle bag. Other than that, I had my weights and the 45-inch TV my dad bought me for my birthday.

I packed my stuff in the car and went back in the house one last time. I set on my bed and fantasized about my future. My Aunt Kim had an extra bedroom at her house in Atlanta for me, and she told me I could stay as long as I wanted to. My strategy was to stay with her for two years.

I already had a job interview lined up. My plan was to start working at the airport while studying to take the GED. I figured to stay working at the airport while attending trade school to specialize in automotive technology. At the end of the two years, I would start my career and move out on my own. I recounted the money I saved, recited a prayer of protection, and left my dad's house for good.

I drove to the shop to say goodbye to my dad. He was sitting down behind the counter when I walked in. I never once saw him sitting down while at the shop. I walked up to him behind the counter and reached out my hand. He stood to his feet and grabbed me for a hug. We exchanged light talk before I hit him with a hard question. "How come you never left E.C. Pops?"

"I never wanted to." His reply was quick and surprising.

"Never?"

"I left once, right before you were born. I was only across the bridge in Chicago, and still I was homesick."

"I don't get it. Why here?"

"Why not here? It's not too big and it's not too terribly small. There ain't a lot to see, but we live close to one of the great lakes. The people are good, and the food is great. Don't get me wrong, Rob, I would love to visit other places. I can't wait to visit you in the ATL. But I'm gonna be buried right here in northwest Indiana. Midwest. U.S.A."

We talked some more and then he gave my car a good check-up. After I left the shop, I went to fill up my tank and then I went to pick up Co-Co. I didn't expect Junior and Dewy to be at Co-Co's house, but they were. In fact, it was quite a bit of people. Everybody was sitting in the shade on the porch chillin and listening to music. Uncle Jeff was manning the grill while his lady friend kept trying to keep the sweat from running down his face. She had two towels.

I was still mad at Junior for stashing that brick in my car at the bowling alley, but I wasn't about to make a scene. I kept it cool. He didn't know it, but him and Dewy were stuck. But Co-Co and I had a way out. I walked up on the porch and greeted each of my boys properly.

No sooner than I found a spot to sit, I was handed a plate of hot food and an ice-cold pop. Respect. It was my first time eating that day, and I ate it all. I had a grilled polish sausage, baked beans, macaroni and cheese, potato salad, spaghetti, and some chips.

After I ate, I kicked it with the crew a little while longer before reminding Co-Co that we had a long drive ahead of us. I followed him in the house to help him with his bags. I made it to his room to discover that he was only half-way packed. He started throwing things into his suitcase while I recalculated our estimated arrival time. When I was done, he talked me into gift wrapping a pair of earrings he bought for his mama.

It was a half-hour later, and we were finally heading to the car with Co-Co's heavily packed bags. When I walked out of the house, I saw Big Mike sitting on the porch with Junior and Dewy. Uncle Jeff was cleaning off the grill.

I looked Big Mike's way and we exchanged, "What's ups?" He had a small grin of approval on his face. The more I kept rejecting his job proposals over the past year, the harder he tried to lure me in. Now it looked like he was finally able to admit defeat. I was ready to show him and the rest of my crew that there was a better way.

We put his suitcase in the trunk and the rest of the bags in the backseat. Junior and Dewy walked us to the car. Uncle

Jeff pulled Co-Co to the side. That's when Dewy started talking trash to me, "You sure about this, JBJ? It ain't too late to change your mind."

"How about you?" I shot back. "We got some room in the backseat still. Y'all tryna roll with us?" I looked at him and then at Junior. They started laughing. "Nah. You got this, JBJ," added Junior.

All in all, it was a decent farewell party. I was tired from all the food and we were three hours behind our original schedule, but we were certainly hitting the road. I was so ready to eat up the miles. Once we made it passed Lafayette on highway 65, the walls were no longer closing in. They were expanding all around me.

As the daylight started to fade, my mind was getting tired. We made a pitstop somewhere outside of Nashville. I refilled the tank and bought an energy drink to help me cross the finish line in Atlanta. I checked over the details of our trip and then I got back on the highway. It was after 9:00 and we were a little past the halfway point.

Co-Co fell asleep less than an hour into the second part of our journey. I had my music on full blast, and he still managed to doze off. The energy drink had me in a beautiful zone. I was cruising at a perfect pace while enjoying the drive and the music. The zone I was in crashed when I noticed that my car was driving funny. Something was definitely wrong with one of my tires.

I pulled over to check it out. The rear tire on the left side of my car was deflating quickly. I instantly remembered the pothole I'd hit when I was getting back on the highway. I got back in the car and turned off the music. I woke up Co-Co and told him to start looking in the glove compartment for the key to my rims. He found the key and gave it to me.

A state trooper pulled up behind me in his cruiser when I was about to get out the car. Instinct made me freeze. The power of fear is remarkable. I was young and determined to make something out of myself. I was riding clean, and a bright future was just ahead of me. I should have held my chin high, but I was scared to the core, my heartbeat was sprinting, and I wanted my mama.

The thought of her distracted me. I pictured her whispering to me and telling me that everything was going to be alright. Her presence comforted me. I put my hands on the dashboard and waited for the state trooper to make the first move. Co-Co did the same. "License and registration, please." So far so good.

I placed the rim key on the dashboard and looked at the officer, "I'm going to reach for my wallet. It's in my pocket." I pulled out my license and registration and handed it to him.

He looked over at Co-Co and then back at me. He directed his next question towards both of us, "Any weapons and or firearms in the car?"

"No," we both answered.

"I see you have a blown tire. How'd that happen?"

"I hit a pothole a while back."

"That's too bad," said the officer. "I'll take a closer look at your paperwork in my car, then I'll be back."

When he left, I checked in on Co-Co. He was almost sweating. I loosened up a little but not completely. I told him that we were good and that we were just a few short hours away from his mama's house.

The officer walked up to my window and gave me my things back. Then he asked if I wanted help fixing my tire. The question was like a coin flip, and it totally caught me off guard. It landed on, "Yeah, that would be cool."

I got the rim key off the dashboard then looked over at Co-Co as I got out the car. He stared at me like I was a baby alien, and I laughed a little on the inside. Co-Co was still tense, but I was willing to accept the help of an officer who wanted to serve and protect.

I gave the rim key to the officer and went to the trunk to get all that was needed to fix the tire. I moved a lot of stuff around until I got to the part underneath the tarp that held the jack, crowbar, and spare tire. There was a black book bag crammed in next to the spare tire. It wasn't my book bag, and it couldn't have been Co-Co's either. His suitcase was in the trunk, but his bags were in the backseat.

I unzipped it and looked inside. There was an instant flashback from the night at the bowling alley. But this time it wasn't just one brick. There were six or seven bricks stuffed in the book bag along with two envelopes filled with cash. So much for riding clean.

I zipped it back up in a hurry. And no sooner than I placed it under Co-Co's suitcase, the officer joined me at the truck and flicked on his ultra bright flashlight. I started pulling hard at the car jack. "I think it's stuck!"

"Let me give it a try," said the officer. Just as he took another step closer, the jack gave way, and I was able to lift it. I handed it to the officer and went back in for the jack and the crowbar.

He provided the light I needed while I worked in silence with a million things competing for my attention in my head. I quickly removed the rim and replaced the flat tire with the doughnut. I tried like hell not to cry, but I was so angry that I started to taste blood. When the job was done, I asked the officer to throw the flat tire in the backseat. While he was securing the tire, I put the jack and crowbar back in the trunk.

"That was a pretty efficient job you did back there, young man."

"Thank you. I'm the son of a really good mechanic, and I'm about to start school for automotive technology." I wasn't telling him that to brag or to have him in my business. I said those words because they were what I needed to hear at that moment.

"Good for you," he replied. He tapped on the top of my car and told me to drive safely.

When the opportunity came, I merged back into traffic. I stayed in the outside lane and drove to the speed limit until the state trooper passed us by. I got off at the next exit and pulled into the parking lot of a motel. I parked in between two cars and let my seat back. We sat there for a while. I broke the news to Co-Co and told him about the bookbag and the envelopes stuffed with cash.

"Big Mike is at it again. He's using us to transport his dope. We need to get rid of it, and then we need to rethink our plan about going to Atlanta."

I stopped talking and waited for Co-Co to respond, but when I looked over at him, his head was turned toward the window like he was in deep thought. I didn't blame him for his silence because it was a whole lot to process.

But then Co-Co turned toward me a few minutes later and said, "Look, bruh, we can't throw away that dope. And those envelopes filled with cash if for us. It's how we start over."

Now it was me staring at Co-Co like he was a baby alien. "Naw, cuz! Don't tell me you knew about this?!"

"Yes, Rob, I did. But it's not a big deal if you look at it the way that I am. Big Mike will have somebody meet us at the park near my mama's house. He ordered me to make the delivery before giving you your envelope. He gave me -his word that it is a one and done for us."

After saying all of this, Co-Co tried to convince me to get back on the highway, but something snapped in my brain. I decided at that moment that I was done with everyone except my dad. The fresh betrayal was almost comical. "Get out my car, Co-Co."

"I can't do that, Rob. Let's go finish this job and get paid, bruh! Don't you get it? Those envelopes are just what we need to start over! Yes, it's dirty money! But it's one job, bruh! One time!"

I hit him in the face with my closed fist. I probably broke his nose, but like I said, I was done. "Get out Co-Co!"

"I'm not getting' out this car! Hit me again if you want to, but I'm not letting you mess this up for us!" Stubbornness runs on both sides of my family, the Black side, and the Puerto Rican side.

I got out the car and started throwing out his bags. Then I popped the trunk and threw out his suitcase. I unzipped the book bag and started flinging bricks across the parking lot like I was Jalen Hurts. That's when Co-Co jumped out the car and tried to rush me. I hit him in the jaw, and he stumbled back.

"What are you doing, Rob," there was a brokenness in his voice. I threw the last brick at him, and he caught it. I got back in the car and pulled off while Co-Co went searching in the dark for the scattered bricks.

I got back on the highway and continued on 75 south, even though I lost all sense of purpose. I knew I couldn't turn around and go home, and I couldn't just show up at my aunt's house either. I started getting a lot of texts messages and calls ten minutes into my drive. But I ignored them all.

I called my dad. It was a long conversation because I had to tell him about all the other times Big Mike tried to force me into his world, but time meant nothing to me anymore. My dad was patiently taking everything in, but he put me on hold to take another call.

As I waited, I thought about the situation I was in. I did not have a backup plan, and I was desperate for a solution. Every single detail about my immediate future was unknown. But I was not defeated.

My dad must have shared my desperation because he came back on the call with half a plan for me. He told me to stay on my current route and not to stop until I was a couple hours south of Atlanta. He told me to find a place to rest for the night and to call him in the morning. Before I ended the call, I asked him about the call he took. He told me that it was Big Mike and that he was looking for me. He didn't tell me anything else.

It was after 4:00 in the morning when I finally got off the highway to rest. I pulled into a low budget hotel and rented a room with cash. I struggled to get comfortable. The walls were grimy, the pipes were loud, and the air was foul and dank.

I woke up early that morning without urgency or direction. I pulled into the gas station for an energy drink, a doughnut, and gas. When I made it back to the car, I called my dad. He gave me an address to put in my phone's GPS and told me to call him when I made it there.

I got off the highway a few hours after entering Florida. I drove along state highways and a lot of back roads before I arrived at my destination late that morning. The GPS prompted me to stop at a small ranch house located in a swamp filled town in the middle of nowhere. With nothing to lose, I walked through the gate and to the front door and then I knocked. I almost cried when Uncle Chad opened the door and invited me in.

I gave him a bear hug. My face must have been painted with surprise because he looked at me and said, "Good to see you too, nephew. We'll talk later. But right now, you need a shower, a sandwich, and a long nap." I called my dad to let him know I'd arrived and then I did everything Uncle Chad told me to do.

When I woke up from my nap, we had a long talk. It turned out that Uncle Chad didn't leave East Chicago without a trace after all. My dad knew where he was all along. Uncle Chad made plans to retire in Florida a long time ago, and they kept his location a secret in case of a situation like this. They didn't trust Big Mike and they knew that he was a predator and would try almost anything to recruit me.

Later that evening, I sat out on Uncle Chad's back porch. I was thankful for the mosquito net that surrounded it. My uncle left to take care of business that night, and I was left alone to create a different plan for my fresh start.

November 21, 2024

I decided that my fresh start is a good thing. It's a lonely thing, but it is a good thing. I miss my dad. We talk every once in a while, but who knows when I'll be able to see him again? I miss Co-Co too, and I often wonder how he's doing.

I'm still getting a decent amount of sleep. It took me some time to get used to the bugs and the geckos that sometimes crawl into Uncle Chad's house. Then there were the thoughts of what life could have been like if I stayed on course to Atlanta. I can honestly say that I'm over those unproductive thoughts.

I also decided that I don't need to look over my shoulder anymore. I had done nothing wrong. Okay, sure. I may have destroyed some of Big Mike's dope when I went on a rampage in the parking lot that night, but that was payback for all the times he tried to pin me. I can truthfully now say that I'm no longer trapped.

With the money I'd brought with me, I got the internet installed. I first had to convince my uncle that the internet was a need and not a want. Being online allowed me to continue with my initial plan. I took and passed the GED and now I'm taking online classes for electric automotive technology. The hands-on training begins next semester, and I can't wait. I work part time at a tire shop doing the same types of things I did up north in my dad's shop.

I officially declare the rambling phase over. After I finish trade school, I'll be ready to start a career with one of the big car companies, or maybe I'll start my own business working with electric cars. My life right now is boring, but it's mine, and it reminds me of a line from my favorite rapper, "There's no such thing as a life that's better than yours." That's exactly how I feel right now. I wonder if Bre ever heard that song before? If not, I'll have to play it for her.

Until next time,

JBJ

The End

| 3 |

GENERATION GAP

ROUND ONE: ANTWON

How could she do this to me? She never would have done this to my sister Monica or any of Aunt Dee's kids. But she singled me out, her youngest grandson.

Granny never had a negative thing to say about me. She never listened to any lies about me either. Her voice was always full of caring and concern. I could never do anything wrong in the eyes of Granny. Not ever!

For the most part, we always lived with my grandma. When I was five, my mama started leaving home for days at a time. Granny didn't mind at first, but I do remember her arguing with my mama one day about staying home and taking care of us.

"Better yet," Granny said, "why don't you get yourself together and get a place of your own. It's about that time."

Mama took Granny's advice and found us a place to live, but it didn't last long. I don't remember much about that tall building, but the apartment was small and cold. Sirens and flashing lights pierced the silent night air. We were okay as long as the noise stayed on the streets and didn't come into the building.

Sometimes my daddy came to stay with us. My daddy is short, muscular, and light skinned. People used to say that my older sister Monica looked just like him. He was always angry and argued about everything. He would stick around for a day or two and then leave. I think he preferred to be with the noises on the streets.

Those were probably the worst months of my young life, and it must have been that way for my mama too. I woke up one morning back in Granny's arms. Mama started leaving more and more after we moved back in with Granny. Now we're lucky to see her a few times during the year. I like it when she comes around for short stays, but I'll never tell her that.

It was Granny who made sure Monica and I stayed in school. I never missed a perfect attendance award in my life! When I was younger and used to get sick, Granny would make me go to school anyway. She would say something like, "Try to make it to the end of the day, Twon. I'll check on you again after school."

Other than that, Granny was cool back then. Everything was whipped cream over a perfectly made strawberry sundae.

Granny started to change once I got to middle school. She started taking sides with Monica and some of my teachers whenever an issue occurred with my name in it. She began to fuss at me more and more. Now she can no longer talk to me without arguing.

This is around the time she started getting annoying too. Granny developed what Monica and I call, *drive through phobia*. She pulled up to the drive through window at KFC one night, and when the girl asked if she could take her order, Granny spoke straight into the speaker and said, "Gravy!"

"Um, would you like food with that Ma'am?" was the girl's response.

Part of me wanted to laugh, while a different part of me wanted to cry. Another part of me wanted to get out the car and walk the rest of the way home. I learned that trying to help during these situations only confuses her and makes matters worse. So, I just slumped down in my seat and avoided eye contact with the girl at the window.

It's hard to understand Granny nowadays. She almost ripped my head off when she found out that it was me who smashed down her slice of homemade caramel cake. I thought it was mine! It's not like her to leave food out in the open. Who in their right mind would leave a deliciously moist piece of homemade caramel cake unattended? She woke me up from a pillow wetting sleep just to give tell me off!

Then she threw me for a loop the very next day. I bumped into the stand that houses a family treasure, a porcelain vase with a gold rim and hand painted with a kente cloth pattern. Inside the vase are the ashes of my Great Grandma, Ida. When I fell into the stand Granny's exact words were, "Be careful, Antwon, baby. We don't want that to fall." Any other time, it would have been instant verbal abuse. I couldn't figure it out.

Granny used to cook once upon a time too. Now she only cooks for Great Uncle Jesse whenever he comes around. And that's not too often. We're left to fend for ourselves most of the time. It's like she stopped caring for us. Then again, Granny has always been nice to Monica. I guess the love lost is just for me.

I still can't believe she kicked me out the house though! I'm only thirteen and she put me out. She never even kicked my mama out the house! I'm glad my friend Sinclair's mom put me up for a few days, but I don't know what I'm going to do after that. Granny, Granny, Granny!

ROUND TWO: GRANNY

That fat-headed big foot grandson of mine is not going to drive me crazy! No, sir, not me. I'm not the one. Whatever happened to the days when all he would do is eat, sleep, and poop on himself? I'd rather deal with changing diapers than to deal with some of the crap that be coming from his mouth.

I'm real appreciative of Ms. Collins for going along with my plan and letting Antwon stay over for a few days. I need this break! I should call and ask if she could make it a full week. But I don't want to impose. I suppose.

Hopefully he'll show some act right when he does come back home. I'm a pretty darn smart woman, but I can't understand for the life of me how a precious boy can go to sleep one night a little angel and wake up on his twelfth birthday the seed of a demon. Okay, I admit, the changes were gradual, but I still don't understand them.

Once Antwon made it to middle school the ship started to sink. The teachers were complaining about his lack of trying and all he did at home was waste time watching videos on his phone or playing video games. On top of all that, he has mastered the annoying art of talking back.

I'll give him one compliment though. He's very watchful and he knows the right buttons to push. And you can talk to him until it hurts, but he still won't get the main idea of the conversation.

On my way out the door one evening, I told him and Monica both not to mess with my slice of homemade caramel cake that Mrs. Palmer brought over for me. I left the caramel cake sitting on my kitchen table and rushed out of the house to pick up a prescription before the pharmacy closed. When I got back home, I ate the dinner that I'd prepared before I left, I turned on the 10 o'clock news in the front room and went to the kitchen to receive my slice of cake. It was gone!

When I looked in the trash can I instantly knew who the perpetrator was. Antwon! When he finished savoring my cake, he made a ball out of the foil and threw it in the trash can. Nobody else makes a ball out of foil but Antwon. I tried to wait until morning to confront him, but it just couldn't wait. I had to get him out of bed and give him a piece of mind for taking my piece of cake.

He's so impatient too! Come on Granny this or hurry up Granny that. *Granny's fist is about to go on top of your head!* That's what I want to tell him.

But what really bothers me is the lack of respect. I'm constantly reminding him to watch his mouth in front of me. When he was five, he used to love to open doors for me in public. Now it's everybody for themselves. And what gets me the most is that feeling of being unappreciated.

I have and will continue to provide for my grandkids. Not because I have to, but because it's the right thing to do. You would think he's old enough to understand this, but apparently, he's not. Antwon, I hope you get your act together, Grandson.

ROUND THREE: COME STRAIGHT HOME

Antwon and Sinclair were forced to take the long walk home from school one October afternoon. They were super busy showing off in front of a group of girls on the other side of the building, and they lost track of time. The buses departed Marshall Middle School at precisely 2:45 p.m. every day.

When they finally arrived at the correct exit ready to load their bus, they witnessed it fade into the distance without them. After kicking up dust they laced up their shoes and prepared for the long walk home, two and a half miles to be exact.

They reached Sinclair's house first. Sinclair cut through his front lawn creating his own path to the front door, but Antwon kept walking. Sinclair looked over his shoulder, "Aren't you staying over again?"

"Nope. My granny sent me a text and told me to come straight home."

"It's about time," Sinclair teased. "I was gettin' sick of sharing my room and my food with you."

"Whateva, man," Antwon replied. "See you tomorrow!"

"Later, Twon!"

Antwon went straight to his room when he made it home. He threw his jacket on the chair and stretched out on his bed. With his arms crossed behind his head, Antwon smiled as he looked around the bedroom at all his belongings. He closed his eyes for a few seconds. When they popped back open, Antwon sat up on the bed, let out a deep sigh, and then he left his room to look for his grandmother.

Her bedroom was toward the back of the house on the opposite side of the kitchen. He gently opened her the door and saw her peacefully at rest on her pillow-filled bed. He crept over to the TV on her dresser and turned the power off. The sudden silence caught her attention, "Is that you Twon?"

"Yeah Granny, it's me."

"We're gonna have us a little talk in the morning. Okay?"

"Okay, Granny," he replied.

ROUND FOUR: THE TALK

Grandma went to work in the kitchen the next morning. Pivoting back and forth from the stove to the countertop, she filled three plates with pancakes, eggs, sausage, cheese grits, and fresh grapes. She called for Monica and Antwon as poured orange juice into three glasses.

She joined her grandkids at the kitchen table then blessed the food. "Don't get too spoiled y'all. I figured I'd make ya'll breakfast for a change instead of havin' you eat that sugar in a box."

"Thanks Granny," Monica replied.

"Yeah, thanks O.G.," agreed Antwon.

"You can thank me by takin' out the garbage without me always beggin' you. It's a shame that you would rather wait on me to take it out."

"And you, Miss Thang," she turned to face Monica, "make sure you take care of these few dishes when you get home this evening."

"Now Granny, you know you never have to ask me twice to do a thing." Monica shot Antwon a shady look.

Not much was said after that. The only sound came from the silverware scraping the bottom of their breakfast plates. Antwon finished his off first. He emptied his scraps in the trash, put his plate, fork, and glass in the sink, and then headed toward the front door with his backpack and gym bag. "See y'all later!"

"Not so fast, Twon!" Grandma yelled. "Come back in here and sit down. Did you forget about our talk?"

"No, I didn't forget," he sat back down. "I figured you wanted to wait until after school."

"No. I said last night that we would talk in the morning and that's exactly what I meant."

Monica finished what was left of her breakfast and put her plate in the sink. She kissed her Granny on the cheek and left for school.

"I'm lettin' you back in Antwon, but things are gonna have to change."

"I know Granny. I don't like arguing with you no more than you like arguing with me. Though sometimes I think you actually like arguing with me."

"That don't make sense, Twon! You think I like raisin' my blood pressure!? Is that what you really think?"

"No, Granny."

"Well, good. I just want you to start pulling your weight around here and stop talking back to me. My heart can't take it much longer."

"Alright, Granny. I hear you. Can I go now? If I miss the bus, you'll have to take me."

"Go ahead, but remember our little talk," she warned.

"I will. And remember I need you to pick me up from practice today at five o'clock, Granny. And please don't be late. Please."

ROUND FIVE: MAN BABIES

It was announced the day before over the loudspeaker that Antwon had made the basketball team. Therefore, the next day went by smooth as silk for Antwon, and the constant grin on his face proved it.

The newly assembled basketball team gathered early in the gym where they congratulated each other with nods of approval and handshakes. Before the coach arrived to start the practice, the boys competed in several activities to determine who was the best in each category.

After practice the steam left the ship. Instead of handshakes and contests to see who could jump and touch the rim there were gasps for air and bodies laid out on the gym floor.

Coach Gates beamed with pride after the first practice. He gazed around the gym and humored himself at the condition the boys were in. "Same time tomorrow man babies but prepare to stay an hour later!"

The coach left the gym and the boys slowly started to peel themselves off the floor. They retrieved their book bags and gym bags and left the building. Most of them sat on the curb and allowed the cool night breeze to blow into their damped shirts. The lucky ones lived within walking distance of the school and would be home in minutes.

One by one the car riders were picked up. Goodbyes were exchanged then heads were turned to greet the next arriving vehicle. Antwon and Sinclair were the last ones left. When

Sinclair's mother pulled up, she offered Antwon a ride home. He turned it down insisting that Granny would be there soon.

She pulled to the curb thirty minutes later. He flopped into the backseat, closed his eyes, and then covered his face with his gym bag.

"How was practice Twon?"

He forced his mouth open, "Fine."

"Did you get the jersey number you wanted?"

"We didn't get our jerseys yet," he answered through his teeth, without moving his lips.

"How many points did you score?"

Antwon closed his eyes even tighter and said to himself, *Go to sleep. Don't answer. Go straight to sleep.*

The slam of the car door awakened Antwon. He followed Granny into the house and locked the door behind them.

Antwon walked to the back of the house and threw his gym bag on the floor in the laundry room. Then he went into the kitchen where his attention fell on the covered-up plate of baked chicken on the stove. He seized a chicken leg, ignored the temptation to put it in the microwave, and immediately went to work on it.

Antwon stood in the refrigerator door. He took a long gulp of juice then snatched a handful of purple seedless grapes before closing the refrigerator door. He forced himself in the shower after that and then collapsed on his bed until the next morning.

Granny had just changed into her nightgown and gone into the kitchen to have a late dinner. She made herself a plate and sat alone at the kitchen table. She went to throw away her scraps and noticed that the garbage still had not been taken out. Granny refused to take it out herself or to ask Monica to do it. Instead, a significant amount of disinfectant spray was released into the air and on top of the trash can. Granny lifted her chin high and then went to her room for the rest of the night.

ROUND SIX: HOT SEWAGE IN A BAG

Monica and Antwon entered the kitchen the next morning to the pleasant surprise of another home cooked breakfast. "Morning Y'all," greeted Granny. Instead of pancakes she whipped milk and butter in a steaming pot of oatmeal.

"Y'all smell that?!" she asked while turning her nose up.

"Euh, I smell it," answered Moncia. "It smells like hot sewage in a bag." She threw Antwon a mean look.

Antwon reversed the dirty look, and then he answered, "I was gonna' say it smells like cinnamon, sugar, and oatmeal."

"No, Monica was right! It is the garbage. And it's sky high too."

"I'll take it out," he surrendered, but he did not move.

While spooning the oatmeal into three bowls at the countertop, she turned her head toward the table to see Antwon seated while rubbing his hands together in anticipation.

"Now I heard you say that you were going to take out the garbage, but your big head is still sitting there in that chair. Now get up Twon'!"

"Right now? I thought you meant when I got home from school."

Grandma turned around with the big wooden spoon cocked back like a hammer, "Antwon Maurice Richardson!" Monica covered her head and ducked for cover.

"I'm just kiddin' Granny! Calm down! I'm moving!"

When he returned to the table, he had a very small amount of oatmeal in his bowl. Granny and Monica snickered at his reaction to the puny portion.

"That's how it's gonna be Granny? You gonna deprive me of food just because I made a tiny mistake? I'm a growin' boy. I need to eat!"

"There's some more oatmeal in the pot if you want some more, but you're the one who started with the jokes this morning."

He went to fill his bowl with more oatmeal. "Are you gonna pick me up on time today, Granny? I got practice until six tonight. And please don't be late this time. Coach Gates be killin' us, and a brotha be ready to go home!"

"If I still got breath and my heart is pumping, I will be there to pick you up."

"Dang Granny," opposed Monica, "why so dramatic?" The table overflowed with laughter then everyone went their separate ways.

ROUND SEVEN: THE FALLOUT

At school Antwon noticed a rise in his stock ever since his name was associated with the basketball team. His approval from the girls was at an all-time high; it fostered hate in the eyes of some of his male peers, but he still regarded it as a positive change. The teachers even gave him a little more slack in class. Instead of the usual one, he was now allowed two interruptions before they gave him the side eye. He even became obsessed with keeping his waves brushed back with his hairbrush.

Antwon was a few minutes late for practice. With a limp in his walk and a humble grin on his face he nodded to everyone he passed on his way to the gym. He knew that once the gym doors closed behind him his super-star status would be over.

Antwon was right. It was like Coach Gates had it in for them. He worked them hard. They did every basketball drill imaginable. He would have pushed them even further if his assistant hadn't pointed out the fact that they were boys on a middle school team and not NBA players.

After practice the boys peeled themselves off the floor and stumbled to the parking lot where they waited for their rides. There was not much talking during the wait. Instead of actually saying goodbye the boys waved before mustering up enough strength to shut the car door behind them. Even the ones who lived in walking distance called home for a ride.

Antwon and Sinclair were the only ones left, again. When Sinclair's ride showed up, he walked to the car then looked back at his friend. He extended his hand as an invitation for a ride home. Antwon waved him off.

What started out as a plea in his mind became a chant thirty minutes later, "Please Granny, show up now." He repeated this over and over again for another thirty minutes.

Without funds or a phone with power, Antwon lifted himself off the curb and started to walk the two and a half miles home. His calf muscles burned with every step he took.

Antwon heard the approaching engine of Granny's car three blocks away from the house. The driver's side window rolled down and she began to speak, "Hey Antwon. Don't be mad at me. Get in the car."

"That's all right, Granny, I'm almost there now."

She pleaded with him a second time, but he waved her off and continued on his solo mission to the finish line. Before walking in the house, he glued his lips shut. He made up his mind that even if Beyonce was in his living room, he would walk right by her without saying a word.

He walked through the living room ignoring his sister who was sitting on the floor in front of the TV braiding her hair. Granny was resting in the recliner with a jar of CBD oil rubbing her legs. Great Uncle Jesse had just managed to sit down on the couch with his walker still in front of him. Antwon went straight into his room and closed the door behind him.

Granny followed behind him and banged on his bedroom door. She continued to bang on the door ignoring her uncle's call, "Leave that boy alone!"

"Stay out of this, Uncle Jesse!" was her reply and she continued to bang on the door.

Antwon gave in and cracked the door, just wide enough to confirm that it was open, "What is it Granny? I'm tired."

"You might be mad at me, but you could have at least greeted your sister and your Uncle Jesse."

He opened the door a little wider. "Hi Monica! Hi Uncle Jesse!" He looked at Granny, "Goodnight."

"Real cute, Antwon!"

"Can I go to bed now Granny?"

"I don't like your attitude, Twon!"

"And I don't like when you make promises you can't keep! I waited over an hour for you to show up. I started to get worried at first after what you said at breakfast this morning. But now I see that you're alive and well!"

"I'm sorry about that Antwon, but don't you even care to hear why I was so late? Anything could have happened to me."

"Like I said, you look fine to me Granny."

"You know what? Boy, you better watch who you talkin' to like that."

"Can I go to bed now?"

"Don't you ever ask me for another ride!" She threw her hands in the air and walked away.

"Don't worry, Grandma. I don't plan to. I'd rather ride home with Sinclair or walk than to wait forever on you!" He slammed his door closed.

After that altercation not a word was shared between Antwon and Granny for quite some time. If there was something to be communicated the message was passed along through Monica.

ROUND EIGHT: UNCLE JESSE

Antwon continued to show up for basketball practice and he rode home with Sinclair and his mother. After practice he stayed over Sinclair's house until ten o'clock at night. By the time he walked into Granny's house, she would already be asleep. When he wasn't eating over Sinclair's house, he would pick off the leftovers in the refrigerator before showering and going to bed.

A day turned into a week, and then one week turned into two weeks. It was on a Friday morning at the bus stop when Sinclair told Antwon that he would have to make different arrangements after school. Sinclair had made plans to stay the weekend with his father.

Antwon was reminded of this after school when Sinclair did not show for basketball practice. After practice Antwon took the long journey on foot to Granny's house.

When he walked through the door, he saw Monica in the recliner on her phone. He also saw Granny and Uncle Jesse sitting on the couch going over some paperwork.

Antwon managed to squeeze out, "What's up y'all," before walking in the direction of his bedroom.

"Hold on there, Young Blood," his Uncle Jesse demanded. "Come talk to your uncle for a second." He pushed his walker to the side of the couch so that Antwon could sit next to him and hold a face-to-face conversation.

"What's going on, Young Blood?" Antwon did not answer. "Your Granny tells me that you two are still not talking. Is that true, nephew?" While waiting for Antwon to answer, he gently grabbed Antwon by the hand.

"Yeah, I guess so. Look, I'm tired Uncle Jesse." Antwon carefully removed his hand from underneath his uncle's. "I'm about to go lay down." Antwon got up and walked away.

Great Uncle Jesse hollered behind him, "But I'm not done yet!" He fought his way off the couch and onto his feet.

Monica was the first to notice his struggle, "Uncle Jesse, NO!"

"Look what you done, Twon!" shouted Granny. "Uncle Jesse sit back down!"

"What are you doin, Unc!" Antwon ran back to help him. "You shouldn't be on your feet!"

"Get off me! I got this!" Uncle Jesse stood to his feet. "Do I have your attention now?"

"You got it."

"And what about you, Gail!?" Uncle Jesse turned his gaze on Granny.

"Yes! You have my attention Uncle Jesse, now please sit back down!"

"I will do no such thing! Not until there's peace in this house! Antwon, you need to grow up nephew! I'm always hearing my niece complaining about you not takin' out the garbage. That's not askin' too much! When I was your age, I took out the garbage, went to school, and held a full-time job. Man up!

And watch how you speak to her, son. Show some respect! Raising you is her choice. You hear me? I said it's her choice. And be patient with her, Twon. Her memory ain't the sharpest, but she remembers to pay the mortgage and keep food in this house.

And you, Gail, stop naggin' at him so much! I'll give you credit because it's hard for a woman to raise a man, especially nowadays. But listen to what he has to say. He ain't a boy anymore! He is a young man. Even if he don't act like it at times!"

No one dared to stop Uncle Jesse when he started walking toward the antique wooden stand that held the family heirloom, the porcelain vase. He held the vase in his unsteady hands and continued, "This is my baby sister Ida in this vase." He paused and kissed the side of the vase. "You think she approves of you two not talking!?" They didn't answer. "Well, do you?"

Granny responded, "No, she don't approve." She then looked skyward, "I'm sorry mama."

"Nope, she don't like that at all," agreed Antwon.

Great Uncle Jesse staggered back to the couch and eased himself down. "Stop all this foolishness!" He looked at Antwon, "Now you made me tired!" Then he looked at Granny, "What's for dinner, Gail?!"

Catfish, baked yams, and collard greens completed the late dinner spread that evening, accompanied by tropical punch kool-aid with sliced lemons. Great Uncle Jesse said the grace and dinner officially began moments later.

"Granny," Antwon acknowledged, "you really know how to welcome a man back home!"

"Uncle Jesse has always been welcomed here," answered Monica.

"Don't feel too lucky Twon, this ain't just for you. We're gonna start eatin' together more often."

"Well, I don't object to that," Great Uncle Jesse noted. "Eatin' a good home cooked meal from you Gail is like winnin' the lottery! You need to train those folks over there at that nursin' home. That's why I'm always tryin' to escape. Unfortunately, these darn legs don't allow me to get too far anymore."

After dinner Monica stayed home and cleaned the kitchen while Antwon rode with Granny to take Great Uncle Jesse back to the nursing home. On the way back home, Granny told Antwon that she contacted her church and sought out counseling for their situation.

"Awe Granny, we don't need counseling. Things ain't that bad. Are they?"

"Antwon, ain't nothin' wrong with asking for help. And don't let anybody tell you anything different. If you ever want something to get better and don't see how to do it yourself, pray over it. I've been doin' a lot of praying since our last falling out and the answer is counseling.

Now I've only been to one meeting. It's a group of three of us grandparents and some of them bring their grandkids with them. Tomorrow is Saturday, and I want you to come with me if you're not doin' anything important that is."

"I got you, Granny. I'll be there."

ROUND NINE: FLAKY DADDIES

Antwon and Monica woke up around 9:00 the next morning and did something they hadn't done since they were little kids. They watched cartoons. Antwon turned the TV off after a while and looked over at Monica, "Uncle Jesse gave it to me and Granny last night. Didn't he?"

"He most certainly did," agreed Monica. Antwon lifted his head off the couch and peeked in the kitchen expecting to see Granny.

"I heard her leave out early this morning," said Monica.

"Can I ask you something big sis?" quizzed Antwon.

"Wuz up?"

"Who you think started that last fall out, me or Granny?"

"To be honest, it was you. You overreacted Twon."

"What?! I asked her to pick me up at six o'clock! I was almost at the door when she finally showed up. You just don't know how tired I was, sis."

"Yeah, but Granny left on time to pick you up. She was in such a rush that she left her phone on the counter. Granny got a flat halfway there and had to walk to the gas station to get help from a man she didn't even know. Granny called me from the stranger's phone and told me to ask Sinclair's mom to pick you up. I tried calling Sinclair's mom, but she never answered."

Antwon put his head in his lap, "I did overreact, and I feel bad."

"It's all in the past," Monica stated. "Don't beat yourself up too bad."

Their conversation was interrupted by the doorbell. They made a quick bet to see who was on the other side of the door.

"My money is on Granny," bet Antwon. "She left out this morning and somehow left her house key."

"My money is on Uncle Jesse," Monica placed her wager. "He got past the security guard and paid a college student $2 to bring him here."

They were both wrong. It was Sinclair on the other side of the door. "What's up Sinclair? I thought you were with your pops for the whole weekend."

"Man! It's a long story. I'll tell you about at the park."

"Cool."

Jamal quickly got dressed, said bye to Monica, and left for the park with Sinclair. Bethel Park was a comfortable place to waste time at on the weekend. People would go there to fish, play basketball or tennis, or just hang out. They found an abandoned picnic table out in the open sun. They pulled it under the shade of an oak tree and sat down.

Sinclair wasted no time spilling the details about his shortened weekend with his dad. "He picked me up early from school yesterday. First time I saw him in like two years. Everything started out fine. We went to a fancy restaurant and had a nice dinner. We talked about my grades and about me makin' the team.

After that we went to his house, and I met his new girl-friend. I told him that I was into hip hop gospel and that I would have to rap for him one day. But he insisted right then that we put in some work in the studio he built in his basement.

I just wanted to kick it with him, but he was takin' this music thing a bit too far. I wish I never opened my mouth. I ended up recording two songs from scratch. He laid down the beats right then and there. We didn't finish until one in the morning."

"Wait a minute, Sin," Antwon interrupted him. "Is Coach Gates your daddy?" They laughed.

Sinclair stopped laughing and looked at Antwon. "And that's not the worst part."

"What else happened?"

"After we recorded the two songs, my dad left the room to take a call. When he came back in, he told me that plans had changed and that he would be leaving town in the morn-ing. He said that his girlfriend would drop me back off at my mama's. He gave me hug, threw me a blanket, and turned the lights off."

"Wow! Just like that?" asked Antwon.

"Yep. Just like that. It's cool though. My expectations are low when it comes to him anyway."

"I feel you, man. I do. I hardly remember what my dad looks like."

Antwon and Sinclair walked to the basketball court and played a few pick-up games. When exhaustion kicked in, they dragged themselves back to the same table they secured in the shade. Antwon and Sinclair stretched out, swatted at the mosquitoes, and watched the maturing sky. That is when Antwon remembered his Granny's words, "I want you to come with me if you're not doin' anything important that is."

Antwon bounced to his feet. "I forgot I was supposed to meet up with my Granny!"

"Go handle that," ordered Sinclair without moving, "I'll catch up with you later."

ROUND TEN: THE RASCAL

On her way to the church, Granny Gail stopped at the gas station. She greeted the attendant at the counter, but his attention was on the door.

"Everything okay?" she asked.

"Yeah. Just a couple of kids that like to cause trouble," the attendant answered. "They come in around the same time every day."

Two of the troublemakers walked into the gas station. The first one was a teenage boy. He had music blasting from his phone. The second one was a teenage girl with a loud voice. She cupped her hands together and yelled out to the attendant, "Wuz up, Havi! You miss us, baby!" The troublemakers walked straight up to the register with a bunch of snacks in their arms.

"Yeah, sure," the attendant answered. "Just hurry up and make your purchase!"

"You heard him, Grandma!" The one with the music blasting pushed his way in front of Granny Gail. He threw a couple bags of chips and some drinks on the counter, demanded some blueberry flavored cigars, and made the purchase. Before the troublemakers left, they looked back at Granny Gail and laughed.

"I'm sorry about that, ma'am," said the attendant. "I guess manners is a thing of the past."

"I guess so," she agreed. Slightly shaken yet determined to make it to the meeting on time, Granny Gail cashed in her scratch-off ticket, filled up her tank, and left.

The meeting was scheduled for 5:00, but Granny Gail walked into the church at 5:15. She caught the elevator down to the meeting room and was hoping to see Antwon fully engaged in the conversation while saving a seat for her.

When she walked into the room everything stopped. Granny apologized for being late and quickly scanned the room. Antwon was not there, but the troublemaker that pushed his way in front of her at the gas station was. The troublemaker stared at Granny through glossy red eyes.

Granny Gail took a seat and looked around again. There were five people in the meeting. There was the soft-spoken counselor, who led the meeting. There were two other women who attended alone. And then there was the rascal from the gas station, sitting next to his angry grandmother.

The meeting was completely dominated by the rascal's grandmother and her cry for help. "Look at him! He doesn't listen to a word I say! And he's high as hell right now! He's worthless, and I don't know what to do about it! He's only here because he was ordered by the court to be!"

When she finished speaking, the other women started to chime in with similar stories. In response to his grandmothers' plea, the rascal started laughing hysterically, and he stared at Granny Gail the whole time. Granny Gail got up and left the meeting.

ROUND ELEVEN: THE CASKET

Antwon ran most of the way to the church. He saw a few cars in the parking lot but neither one of them belonged to his Granny. He still entered the church to search for her. He spotted two deacons walking down the hall and asked them about the meeting. They told him that the meeting had already ended.

On his way out the church, he spotted a longtime friend named Jerrod. He was sitting on a bench by himself. Antwon went over to greet him, but he instantly knew that something was not right with his friend. Jerrod's body was like a statue, and his face was lost in sorrow.

"What's up Jerrod? You good?"

"Nope. I am not good." Jerrod answered without looking at Antwon.

"What's going on?"

Jerrod ignored his question and asked one of his own, "Will you walk up there with me?"

"Where?"

Ignoring his question again, Jerrod stood up. "Yeah. That would be good. Please walk up there with me."

Antwon followed Jerrod down the main hall. Jerrod stopped at the double glass door and looked at Antwon for the first time, "Please walk with me."

Looking through the glass door and into the main sanctuary, Antwon clearly understood what Jerrod was asking. Antwon opened the doors and gently placed a hand on his friend's back. He walked with him into the empty sanctuary, down the long aisle, and up to the open casket.

The woman at rest in the coffin was Jerrod's grandmother. She laid there peacefully like a wise queen. Contentment pierced through the faint smile on her face. Antwon's heart skipped a beat as he imagined Granny Gail laying there in a casket in the essence of a queen. The sudden premonition of his grandmother's death bothered him greatly.

Antwon snapped out of his personal thoughts when Jerrod started to sob. The rest of Jerrod's family approached unnoticed. Jerrod's grandfather pulled him in for an embrace and Antwon quietly exited the sanctuary and then the church.

ROUND TWELVE: THE SILENT TRUCE

Antwon walked into the dark and quiet house with his head down. He took out the garbage and then ate a plate of leftover spaghetti. He then took a long shower while practicing the apology he planned to recite for being a no show at the meeting his Granny desperately wanted him to attend with her.

After his shower he walked into the kitchen for something to drink. His attention was grabbed by a big slice of pineapple upside down cake that was on showcase in the center of the kitchen table. He thought about going in for a pinch but froze when he saw the post-it note next to it. *Hands Off! This means you, Twon!* With his hands raised in a surrendered position, he slowly back away from the table.

"Go ahead," offered Granny Gail who had been watching him all along from the living room.

"Oh, hey Granny. That's all right."

"Will you have some, if I have some with you?" She joined him in the kitchen and gathered two forks and poured two glasses of cold milk.

They savored the cake together. Before they finished it off, Antwon found himself speaking, "Granny, I really wanted to make it to that meeting tonight. I'm sorry. I forgot about it until the last minute." Antwon broadened his shoulders and prepared for the rebuttal.

"That's all right, Twon." Granny Gail brushed it off. "It makes me happy just to know you wanted to make it."

Antwon wanted to ask, *is that it?* But he decided against it. He sat and enjoyed a quiet moment with his Granny.

After they devoured the slice of pineapple upside down cake, Granny Gail ran some dish water and cleaned up the crumbs. Antwon pushed in his chair then walked over to her at the sink. He kissed her on the cheek and whispered, "I appreciate everything you do."

THE END

| 4 |

UNTITLED IN THE WOODS

It was late summer, the last week in July to be exact, when Lylah flopped in the backseat of the family's truck. After scrambling through her bookbag to locate her blanket and headphones, she buckled her seatbelt and exhaled. As the tunes filled Lylah's ears, she closed her eyes and gave a crooked smile as she tried to find the right zone. She was ready to get out of Indianapolis, even if only for a few days, yet she was hesitant about taking a long road trip with her dad and stepmother.

She came out of her zone ten minutes later when the car door on the opposite side swung open. Her stepmother, Natalie, strapped baby Dominic into his car seat, gave Lylah a simple wave, and then left to get her bags for the road trip. Her dad, Jermaine, came to the car a few minutes later. He asked for Lylah's help with packing the trunk, but she turned the volume up on her phone and pretended to be invisible instead.

Once the truck was packed and the business under the hood all cleared, they were ready for the six-hour journey to a vacation cabin in east Tennessee. Her dad and stepmother got in the car and continued their loud debate over something old and boring as Lylah would put it. Their tone and laughter bothered her. And so did Natalie's words when she looked in the backseat and screeched, "Y'all ready to go kiddos?"

Lylah looked over at her nine-month-old baby brother, and all the resentment she had towards her dad and stepmom dissolved. Dominic's gorgeous brown face and big brown eyes were focused on her. He was speaking to her in wet baby babble, and it forced a full smile on her face. Lylah played with him until he tired and then she found herself alone again in search of a new zone.

They stopped at the gas station after a couple hours on the road. Jermaine pulled into a parking spot and rolled all the windows down. Natalie rushed out of the car with baby Dominic. The smell of his dirty diaper was overpowering and required immediate attention. Jermaine and Lylah got out the car too, but Jermaine pulled Lylah to the side before they went into the gas station.

They stood with arms folded resting against the hood of the truck. Jermaine spoke up first, "You need to try and relax during this get-a-way, Ly."

"Yea, dad. Whatever."

"See. That's it right there." He waited for a few people to walk by and then he continued, "That's what I'm talking about, Ly," his tone turned easy. "Put the attitude away. You don't need it. We're a family and everything is good."

"I didn't mean to say it with an attitude. I was just agreeing with you."

"Alright, Ly." He turned to face her. "Look. From this point on, do you think you can be a little nicer to me and to Natalie? I want us to have a good time. There's nothing to fight about baby girl."

With fingers crossed behind her back, she sighed, "Yea dad."

"Good! And thank you." He pulled out his wallet and gave her a twenty. "Now go inside and get some snacks. We still got a long drive."

Lylah went into the gas station for something sweet, spicy, and salty. Her dad's words started to echo in her ear while she was shopping, *"There's nothing to fight about. Be a little nicer to us. Let's have a good time."* She paid the clerk and hurried back to her spot in the truck. She put on her headphones then switched from her playlist to KickToc. She no longer heard the words from her dad's peptalk but only the sounds of the hilarious scenarios that played out in front of her.

Her humorous zone came crashing down when her dad and stepmother came back to the car. Lylah tried to recapture the comical zone when they got back on the highway, but she could not. With her headphones still on, she stared blankly at the screen on her phone and caved into the first demand of her dad's pep-talk, *"You need to try and relax during this get-a-way"*.

Well, no duh! She thought. *Why in the hell would I agree to this vaca if I didn't want to try and relax?* Lylah took a deep breath and then she remembered the promise she made to herself about relaxing and pressing the reset button. Her goal was to make it through the summer and emerge as a new person with a new title at the start of her freshman year.

Lylah suffered a tragic loss at the beginning of her seventh-grade year, and that tragedy made middle school a complete disaster. By eighth-grade, Lylah fell into a pattern of absentee-ism and depression. She had been reprimanded several times for smoking weed in the bathroom during passing periods and for vaping it in class. Despite her numerous challenges, Lylah maintained decent grades and held on to what her school counselor told her, "You are young and bright, Ly, and it is not too late to get extra counseling for what you've been through, to heal from it, and to move forward toward your dreams."

Move forward toward your dreams. Lylah pondered those words. She did not have a dream, but she knew that she would one day and that nothing would get in her way of making that dream come true. Lylah took off her headphones and listened to the 90's R&B music that was bumping through the speakers of the truck. She found comfort and joy in the rhythm of the songs. She hummed along to the catchy melodies until she drifted off to sleep.

The sensation of stillness awaked Lylah. After another pitstop, she read a book to Dominic and secretly shared her junk food with him. Lylah played with him through the sugar rush then rubbed his tummy until he nodded off. She watched videos on Gotube until the low power icon appeared at the top of her screen. She then read her anime book until they finally pulled off the highway and entered the small town in eastern Tennessee.

The sky was overcast and there was a thick fog in the air. Jermaine checked his phone and reported that they should arrive at the cabin in 30 minutes. At Natalie's suggestion, they pulled into a general store to get groceries. Lylah took a good look around at their surroundings after Jermaine parked the truck. They were on the main road, but there was barely any traffic.

Once she was in the store, Natalie shared the shopping list with Jermaine, and they quickly set off to accomplish the task of acquiring groceries. With squinted eyes and an opened mouth, the clerk followed their movements from behind the counter. Lylah held Dominic in her arms. She stayed at the front of the store and watched the clerk.

When they were done with the shopping, they huddled at the cash register. As the clerk was ringing up the groceries, he looked at Jermaine and asked, "Y'all not from around here, are you?"

"What gave it away?" Jermaine asked.

The clerk started to laugh. "You're funny."

"Of course, I am," teased Jermaine, "I'm a comedian."

"Are you joshing me?" asked the clerk.

"If I was joshing you, you'd be laughing already." They both laughed, but Jermaine stopped when he read the look on Natalie's face.

After Jermaine paid for the groceries, the clerk spoke up again, "They shouldn't have rented that cabin to y'all. Some people'll do anything for a buck. And it's a shame really. Best of luck to y'all."

"You have a good evening, man," finished Jermaine.

They piled back in the truck and locked the doors. "What was that about?" Natalie asked.

"That was a little weird, huh?" Jermaine followed.

"Was the clerk a racist or was he trying to scare us?" asked Natalie.

"Or maybe he was trying to warn us," Lylah chimed in.

"I don't know, but I'm tired and hungry just like my little man back there. Let's get to the cabin and settle in." Jermaine pulled back onto the main road toward the cabin.

"Or he could've been talking about the weather," offered Lylah. "The app on my phone shows rain coming to this area."

"I thought you looked at the weather ahead of time, hun?" asked Natalie.

"I did. And no rain was expected."

"How long ago was that, Jermaine?"

There was a pause. "About a week and a half ago."

"Really, hun?"

"It will probably rain for a short while, and then it'll be back to blue skies. Besides, we're here now and we should make the best of it."

The navigation system had them turn off the main road. The first turn led to a road that was narrow and snakelike, and it became increasingly rugged as the elevation increased.

The second turn led to a sharp upwards slope that the truck's engine reluctantly tolerated. The navigation system stopped working and gave them all a sudden scare. Jermaine did not know the direction of the next turn. But when he finally made it to the top of the slope there was only one direction to go, and so he turned left.

The last road was paved with cement, but still it was a road of tight curves and obstacles. Jermaine maneuvered past two cabins on the way to theirs. They were a half mile apart and seemed to be unoccupied. Lylah was the first one to point out their cabin when it came into view. Jermaine parked the truck and then confirmed the name of the cabin, Sacred Solitude.

* * *

Lylah got out the truck and stretched. She looked around at their secluded surroundings. The cabin was small and rustic with a wrap-around porch. There was a large grill on one side of the cabin and a fire pit on the other. A deep green from the colossal trees painted the thick forest all around her. After twirling in a circle, Lylah looked up above the trees at the tall gray sky.

Sacred Solitude was made up of two bedrooms, one bathroom, and a spacious combo room that included the kitchen, dining room, and living room. Lylah was content with having a bedroom to herself and access to the wrap-around porch.

Except for baby Dominic, the family worked as a team to disinfect all surfaces and unload the truck. Lylah played with Dominic while Natalie unpacked the groceries and washed the pots and pans. Jermaine searched the cabin for any signs of faultiness. The stove was broken and neither one of the cabin's three TVs worked. Jermaine tried to report the issues to the maintenance department, but the reception was spotty. The line went dead after a brief ring and a pause.

They devised a quick plan to get through the night without the stove or the TVs. Jermaine kept calling maintenance. He was prepared to drive back into town the next day if the service continued to fail. Natalie rolled up her sleeves and headed to the fire pit and Lylah reluctantly joined her.

Natalie and Lylah searched around the sides of the cabin for sticks. By the end of their search, they had a three-foot pile of timber next to the pit. Natalie used the smaller twigs for kindle to start the fire. Then she showed Lylah how to build and maintain the fire by layering the sticks as they gradually increased in size.

Lylah then followed Natalie into the kitchen. They washed their hands then began putting chopped chicken, broccoli, and potatoes on top of sheets of aluminum foil. Natalie sprinkled on salt and pepper and then folded the foil around the food. They took the food pouches out to the pit and set them around the edge of the fire.

It was good to finally sit still again. The sky was getting darker, but they did not seem to mind. Dominic could not look away from the mystery of the glowing embers and neither could Natalie, who held him tightly while swaying back and forth. Jermaine set in reflective mode while staring through the flames. Lylah looked up at the small window of a sky, while taking note of the dim star clusters that sneakily appeared through the rapidly passing dark clouds. The mood was cozy, and the sound of raw nature was hypnotizing.

The family's peaceful time at the fire pit did not last long. The rapidly fleeing dark clouds ushered in impatient storm clouds. The raindrops that fell on them were so heavy, you could hear them implode when they hit the skin. Lylah led the race from the pit to the cabin. She tucked her phone, tossed the tongs to Jermaine, and made a dash. Natalie was in second place. She threw down the poker, secured Dominic on her hip, and fled. Jermaine was last but still made good time. He grabbed the dinner plate, scrambled through the flames with the tongs, retrieved the four food packs, and then he sprinted to the cabin while balancing the family's dinner.

The storm brought violent wind, magnificent lightning bolts, sporadic thunder, and terrible rumbles. They changed into dry clothes then met up in the combo room for dinner. The foil packs were an experiment for Lylah and Jermaine, but they could not deny how delicious the food tasted. Natalie was in the middle of bragging about the tricks she learned as a girl scout when the cabin went completely dark.

Jermaine used the flashlight in his phone to locate the wall switch. He flicked the switch off and then on, but nothing happened. Natalie used her flashlight to retrieve the scented candle she brought with her. Under the lavender scented flame, the family finished their dinner in silence. They turned off their phones to conserve power and decided to leave the lit candle in the combo room, only to be moved if someone had to take it with them to the bathroom.

Lylah used her flashlight one final time to settle into her room. With the glow from her phone, she spotted the bed, a nightstand, a small dresser, and a window. Lylah walked over to the window and raised the blinds. She put the light up to the window but saw nothing but black. Lylah got under the covers and turned off the flashlight. Her phone was powered to 35%. She shook her head in disbelief and turned the phone off.

With eyes bucked, Lylah could not make out any shapes, nor could she see her own hand waving in front of her. Occasionally, she was able to make out traces of the blinds whenever there was a streak of lightening. The rain was merciless. It continued to pound against the windows while the rumbles of thunder shook the cabin.

"You need to try and relax during this get-a-way." Her dad's words came back yet again. But this time she was ready for them. Lylah smiled. Even though the storm was epic in scale and her family was totally off the grid, she decided to relax. The commotion that was happening was a sign of better times to come. She was looking forward to a great start to her freshman year and a new title to go along with it. Lylah lay in the bed with her hands crossed behind her head. All she had to do was make it through the storm.

The chaos that she tucked in last night was back with vengeance the next morning. Murky daylight spilled through the blinds as the family scrambled to gather their belongings. The rain had not let up, the power was still out, there was no cell service, and a flood awaited them outside. The plan was to call it quits, retreat, and count on a more reliable family getaway in the fall.

During the scramble to leave, all tensions were starting to boil. Dominic was unhappy and cried nonstop and this caused Natalie to be on edge. All Natalie could think about is how her husband, who named himself the navigator, had not checked the weather forecast prior to the trip.

Jermaine's optimism drowned in the six inches of mud water that surrounded the cabin. He was rattled by the baby crying and by the dirty looks that he got from Natalie. What really worked his nerve, however, was the forethought that the truck's engine would not start due to the standing water.

Lylah could not calm Dominic down. Her silly faces and tickles meant nothing to the disgruntled baby. She was also upset because the trip was a failure, and she would not have a new title to start her freshman year. But what really bothered her was her phone. Sometime in the middle of the night, she plugged it into the wall just in case the power came back on. And because of that, her power dropped from 35% to 25%.

Lylah ducked away from the argument that Jermaine and Natalie were having in the combo room. She secured her place in the truck for the return trip home. Lylah covered up with her blanket and put her headphones on for comfort. Her chances of catching a vibe crashed when Dominic, still in the hollering mood, was buckled in next to her. On top of that, the argument that she tried to avoid escalated when Jermaine and Natalie got in the truck.

Natalie found a map in the cabin and wanted Jermaine to use it to get them to the nearest highway, but Jermaine thought it was a terrible idea. He wanted to guide them back to the highway by retracing his steps. Lylah understood what they were arguing about, but she did not care. She only wanted to escape the crying and the bickering. She turned on her phone and did a quick search for her favorite song. She turned the volume way up and hoped that by the time the song was over, they would be in motion with the baby sleep and the adults giving each other the silent treatment.

Natalie gave up on the argument then ripped the map in half. She rolled it into a giant ball and threw it over her shoulder. It landed on Dominic's lap. Completely captivated by its sudden appearance, Dominic stopped crying and instantly started playing with his new favorite toy. Tensions started to ease when the crying stopped.

The adults got out the truck at the same time. Natalie went back in the cabin to use the bathroom and Jermaine got out to look under the hood. He was relieved that the engine started but troubled by the funny sound that it made. Dominic dropped the paper ball on floor and started to whine. Lylah quickly bent down to pick it up. That is when she remembered that her charger was still plugged into the wall in the cabin. She used her blanket as a shield from the rain and rushed back inside for the charger.

Lylah unplugged the charger then remembered the pocket-knife she stashed in the dresser. She bought it from one of the gas stations they stopped at on the way to the cabin. The pocketknife was an instant keepsake. It reminded Lylah of her mother. The handle was blood orange and had a white cloud airbrushed in the middle of it. Two blue monarch butterflies were painted in the cloud. Her mother's favorite color was blood orange and she loved blue butterflies.

Lylah stuffed the charger in her front pocket and put the pocketknife in her back one. She made a cloak out of the wet blanket and braced herself for a sloppy run back to the truck. When she stepped out onto the porch, her heart skipped a beat. The truck was gone and so was her family.

* * *

Lylah ran into the middle of the road hoping that her dad would catch a glimpse of her through his rearview mirror, but the truck was nowhere to be seen. She ran back to the porch and turned on her phone. She tried to call him, but the attempt was useless. Lylah collapsed in the rocking chair and crossed her arms.

Jermaine always made the same face whenever he made a mistake. His mouth would twitch to the side and his eyebrows would fold upward creating identical arches. Lylah pictured him pulling up, rolling down the window, and making that face. Ten minutes passed and she was still waiting to see that face. She figured that he somewhere stuck in the mud after trying to make a U-turn.

Her damp clothes started to itch against her skin, so she went back into the cabin to dry off. After several tries, she remembered the four-digit code to unlock the door. She used a face towel to dry her arms and legs. Then she grabbed the comforter from off the bed and wrapped herself in it. On her way back to the rocking chair, she grabbed an unopened box of cereal.

After an hour of waiting, Lylah's heart started to beat faster. She turned her phone back on and tried to call again. Lylah stepped off the porch after the rain let up, in a failed attempt to catch a signal in the middle of the road. After the second hour of waiting, her surroundings began to close in on her. Lylah felt small, like Dominic, but unlike her baby brother, she was helpless.

Lylah did not have a plan for the dilemma she was in, nor did she know what to do. Her only thought was to wait it out. And then she remembered the candle that Natalie left in the cabin. The dancing flame and the scent of lavender could have brought her instant comfort, but it was not to be. The code reader jammed, and Lylah no longer had access to the inside of the cabin.

After the third hour of waiting the heavy rain returned and tears started to race down her cheeks. Her dad's pep-talk from the day before pierced through her empty thoughts and ignited her rage. "We're a family and everything is good." *Everything is not good.* She thought. *You left your only daughter stranded in the woods.* "Can you be a little nicer to me and to Natalie?" *How about being nicer to me, dad? Can you please come get me?* "I want us to have a good time." *Does this look like a good time to you? This is far from a good time.* "There's nothing to fight about." Lylah screamed, *"This is worth fighting about! I am worth fighting about! Come and get me so we can fight!"*

Lylah's tears dried but the anger grew. She concluded that it was their plan all alone to abandon her in the woods. They either wanted her to find her own way home and learn a lesson in the process, or they wanted her to die like her mother did and never return. Their motives were clear. Her dad was sick and tired of yelling at her about the new person she had become. Jermaine developed a special look of disappointment that was only for her. And Natalie was sick and tired of the embarrassment. As a sixth-grade math teacher at the same middle school, Natalie cringed every time Lylah's name was called over the loudspeaker to report to the office.

Lylah's face was starting to get cold, and she desperately wanted to be inside the cabin before nightfall. She walked around the porch and tried to lift open every window, but there was no such luck. Lylah fell back into the rocking chair and wrapped the comforter around her. She stared blankly out into the storm.

The night came suddenly, and it surrounded her. The loud claps of thunder and frequent ripples of lightning only highlighted the vast darkness. Lylah tried not to think. Formulating thoughts would bring awareness to her situation and that would ultimately lead to fear, and she did not want to be afraid. Lylah's attempt to suppress fear, however, only released her mind to focus on the one thing she feared the most, revisiting her mother's death.

Lylah tried frantically to stop her mind from falling into the abyss, but she was not strong enough. Her thoughts shifted into autopilot, and she became paralyzed. It was a Tuesday afternoon. She had just chosen the country of South Korea to do a presentation on when her social studies teacher called her to his desk. Mr. Pierce handed her a pass and told her that she was leaving for the day.

She said bye to her friends, went to her locker, and met her dad in the office. When Lylah asked where they were going, Jermaine pulled the car over and faced her. He told her that there was a mass shooting at the coffee shop her mother goes to every morning. Tasha's car was parked outside the coffee shop, but she was not answering her phone. The investigators did not know if Tasha was among the survivors or the deceased. Jermaine told Lylah that they were on their way to a meet up location for more details.

They waited in the auditorium of a banquet hall with a lot of other anxious people. Half the people were escorted to a private meeting room without explanation. When they left the private room, they filed out of the banquet hall. Lylah and Jermaine were with the remaining group of people escorted to the private meeting room. They were told that their loved ones did not survive.

Lylah's mind tried to revert to the present, but she fought against it. Lylah screamed out, "Not yet, God! I want to know! I need to know!" A crackle of thunder shook the porch, then Lylah's mind took her back to the evening before her mother was killed.

Lylah was stretched out on her bed and lost in her phone. Her mother opened the door and walked in. She tossed Lylah a Tupac t-shirt, "We keep getting our Pac shirts mixed up. That one's yours."

"Thanks, mama."

Tasha was about to leave but she turned back to face Lylah. She stood in the middle of the room and asked, "You know what Ly?"

"What's up?"

"I'm proud of you."

Lylah looked surprised. "Why?

"Because. You're getting good grades. You're a joy to be around, unlike most teenagers. And you help out around here. You're doing your thing, future queen. And I see you."

"Aww. Thanks, mama. ILY!"

"ILY too, boo!"

Lyla's mind instantly reverted to the present. Tears of joy rushed down her face and a flash of lightning appeared in the sky. It caused Lylah to blink and when she opened her eyes there was a vision of her mother standing in front of her.

Paralysis took over again as Lylah stared at her mother. Tasha stood just as she had in her daughter's bedroom the evening before she was killed. She wore the same blood or-ange nightgown. She smiled at Lylah and then she spoke. "I'm still proud of you, Ly. Now it's time to rest because tomorrow you will save them." Another flash of lightning appeared in the sky, the same place as before. Lylah was alone again.

As she gazed out into the relentless storm, Lylah thought about Jermaine, Dominic, and Natalie. She refused to imag-ine the type of trouble they were in. Still wrapped in the comforter, Lylah curled into the fetal position and laid on the porch. She relished every word her mother said to her during their last conversation.

* * *

Lylah climbed out of her sleeping spot and emerged into a different world. The bright blue sky was littered with motionless clouds. An assortment of deciduous trees outlined the landscape as far as the eyes could see. The soundtrack of the forest was upbeat and lively. For a lengthy moment she soaked it all in, and then she exhaled with hope and a purpose. Her plan was to get to the main road and call 911 for help.

She dropped the comforter, twisted her braids into a long rope, then stepped off the porch. Sacred Solitude was situated in a cul-de-sac surrounded by the forest, and the only way out was in reversal. Before leaving the site, Lylah noticed three unopened bottles of water floating in the fire pit. They were left there the other night when the family ran to the cabin to escape the downpour. Lylah gulped down one bottle and stuck the other two down her shorts.

The ground water started to recede. By the time she made it to the first curve, she was splashing through half an inch of rainwater. It only took her a few minutes to make it to the cabin that was closest to Sacred Solitude. Lylah shivered from the eeriness of it. She wondered just how far she was from the nearest person, and then it occurred to her that she might not want to know the answer. Lylah walked by the second abandoned cabin, and it too was unnerving and void of human activity. She walked faster.

The paved surface ended a hundred feet before the road turned. Lylah navigated the terrain cautiously, but she could not avoid the chunky gravel or the steep drop. Lylah turned her ankle and hit the ground. The pain followed immediately and so did her cry of distress. Lylah closed her eyes and gritted her teeth. She rubbed her throbbing ankle and took deep breaths. Lylah yelled out in agony when she stood to her feet. She screamed with every step she took until the pain became a part of her. Lylah scavenged through the brush along the side of the road until she found a stick long and sturdy enough to guide her down the rocky slope.

The painstaking descent lasted for about an hour before Lylah stopped. She sat on a huge log, took a long drink of water, and ate a few handfuls of cereal. The shade of the forest was cool and welcoming. Lylah stretched out her leg and rubbed her ankle. It had swollen even more since the last time she checked on it. Lylah braced herself for the effort it was going to take her to stand, but her concentration was interrupted by the sound of snapping branches. Right as she turned to where the sound was coming from, the trees parted. A black bear sprang forth through the woods directly across the path from her. Lylah froze.

She made eye contact with the bear and lost all hearing except for the pounding of her heartbeat. It was not a giant bear nor was it a baby. Lylah tried to look away from it, but she could not. The bear showed no interest in Lylah and walked away in the opposite direction. The bear crossed over to the same side of the road Lylah was on and then it disappeared into the woods.

Lylah continued her journey with a new respect for nature and the creatures in it. The second turn offered another decline and hinted that she was one step closer to getting off the mountain and onto the main road. The new path was rockier than the last one, but it had leveled out and allowed Lylah to see in the distance. She spotted her dad's truck half a mile ahead of her. She held in her excitement and kept the same steady pace.

The license plate had been stripped off her dad's truck, but the colt's window sticker and Dominic's car seat were still intact. The doors were left open, and their bags had been ransacked. The truck was facing in the direction of Sacred Seclusion, but the front tire was stuck in mud. Lylah scratched her head when she noticed a second set of tire tracks. She took out her phone but still there was no reception. Tears of frustration seeped freely down her face. Lylah thought about the warning her mother had given her, and then continued the trek towards the main road.

Lylah traveled the same road for about a mile. She paused at the sight of a hidden driveway. It appeared out of nowhere and fresh tire tracks indicated that a vehicle recently entered or exited the driveway. Lylah closed her eyes and thought about her options, and then she thought about her family. She opened her eyes then followed the driveway to see where it led.

The driveway was narrow and curvy. After a fifteen-minute hike along the edge of it, Lylah was able to see where the driveway ended. She paused at the clearing and surveyed the area. At the end of the path was a newly built cabin. It was small and isolated with no signs of life except the fresh tire marks that led away from it.

Lylah heard the faint sound of crying. She scanned the woods, but she could not tell where the sound was coming from. She crept closer toward the cabin but then stopped in her tracks and listened. It was Dominic's cry that captured her attention and it was coming from inside the cabin. Lylah's entire body shook with fear. She pulled her shorts down and squatted to pee just in time. After she finished, she clutched the walking stick and hobbled toward the cabin.

Lylah took her time climbing the steps. She gazed around the porch, hoping to get a peek inside, but the blinds were closed. The door had a deadbolt lock but no keypad. She turned the knob and the door crept open.

Lylah's knees buckled when she walked into the cabin. Dominic was laid out on a dirty sleeping bag in the middle of the floor and Natalie was gagged and tied to a wooden chair. The unfinished cabin smelled of the fresh lumber pile that was stacked against the back wall. There were no rooms in the cabin, only chairs, dirty sleeping bags, and a junk pile.

Lylah dropped the stick and hurried over to Dominic. She picked him up, and he clutched his little arms tightly around her neck. Lylah limped over to Natalie and ripped the duct tape off her face.

"Listen to me, Ly," Natalie ordered once she recovered. "You gotta put the baby down, so that you can free my hands. And everything we do from this moment forward we have to do it in a rush. They'll be back soon!"

Lylah did not want to put Dominic down, but she took Natalie's evenly spoken words to heart, and she snapped into action. She pried Dominic's hands from around her neck and set him on the floor next to Natalie. Lylah used her pocketknife to cut the ropes that held Natalie's hands and feet together.

Natalie stood up and rubbed her wrists. She grabbed Dominic then looked at Lylah, "Let's get your daddy and get the hell out of here!"

Natalie led her to a walking path on the side of the cabin. They followed the path to a tool shed. They opened the shed and found Jermaine unconscious and tied to a wooden chair. His mouth was bound with duct tape. They took turns shoving his arms until he woke up. When he came to, Jermaine's eyes shot open, and he tried to talk through the duct tape.

Natalie peeled the tape off his mouth and Lylah used her pocketknife to free his arms and legs. Once he was out of the restraints, Jermaine stumbled out of the chair and caught himself from falling. They ran back to the porch as fast as they could.

Jermaine took off his tank top and wrapped it around Lylah's swollen ankle. Natalie disappeared into the cabin and returned with Lylah's walking stick. They all started the journey down the driveway toward the road. Jermaine ordered them to keep walking, but he ran back into the cabin.

He smashed one of the chairs into pieces. He used the chair leg to rummage through syringes and broken pieces of glass that were mixed in with the pile of junk. Jermaine collected a plastic bag that contained their bank cards, his license plate, and the keys to his truck. Jermaine sprinted back to his family and revealed a plan to escape down the mountain.

After he shared the details of the plan, Jermaine cut across the driveway and sprinted towards the direction of the truck. He slowed his pace when he made it to the road. Jermaine kept close to the tree line and ran like he was on a treadmill programmed to the highest incline possible.

Lylah and Natalie vanished into the woods before they reached the road. Their waiting spot was twenty yards inward from both the driveway and the road. They were close enough to hear anyone passing by but far enough in the woods not to be seen. Lylah sat on the ground and hoisted her sore ankle on top of a big rock. Natalie sat next to her and nursed Dominic. While they waited for Jermaine to arrive in the truck, Natalie told Lylah everything that happened from the moment they accidentally left her at Sacred Seclusion.

* * *

Dominic dropped the paper ball and started crying. Jermaine looked over his shoulder to get Lylah's attention, but she was not in the truck. They were still on the paved road when he noticed, but the road was too narrow to make a U-turn and it was too curvy to drive in reverse. Jermaine pulled out his phone to call Lylah, but there was no signal.

He continued to drive until he found enough room to make a U-turn. That moment came several minutes later.

The front wheel on the passenger side sank down in the mud when he tried to complete the 180-degree turn. Jermaine tried for over an hour in the downpour to free the tire, but the situation was only getting worse. He climbed back in the truck and shook his head in defeat. Jermaine and Natalie debated their options. They agreed to hike back up to the cabin where Lylah was after the rain eased up.

Three morons pulled up behind them in a red four-door sedan with oversized wheels. Two men in black t-shirts and baseball caps got out the car and approached the driver's side window. Jermaine rolled down his window to greet them. He refused their help and rejected their small talk. The two men walked back to their car, but they did not pull off. They waited.

Jermaine watched them through his rear-view mirror. The waiting game lasted over an hour, and Jermaine started to cuss. He punched the dashboard and then he opened his door. Jermaine ignored Natalie's plea and got out of the truck to confront them. The men were already walking towards Jermaine and one of them had a shotgun. The man with the shotgun aimed it at Jermaine and he froze. He looked at Jermaine and said, "Y'all some fancy folks out here in open country. And just for that, y'all gonna pay."

The other man walked over to Natalie and opened her door. Jermaine and Natalie, with Dominic in her arms, were forced to stand in the middle of the road while a third member of their team, a scrawny lady in a sundress and a cowboy hat, searched the truck for anything of value. When she was done pillaging, they all piled into the sedan. Jermaine was forced to sit next to the driver, and the man with the shotgun sat in the backseat behind Jermaine.

They worked quickly to separate Natalie from Jermaine. The men marched him to the shed, and the lady waited in the car with Natalie and Dominic. The men came back min-utes later and forced Natalie into the unfinished cabin. They gagged her and tied her to the chair, and the scrawny lady picked up Dominic and held him in her arms. She rubbed his back and whispered to him, "Mama's got you baby boy!"

The morons were squatters. They were talking about mov-ing on after the storm. Natalie watched them move carelessly around the cabin drinking beers and sipping whiskey. Once the rain eased up, they started talking about their intentions with Natalie and Jermaine.

One of the men went by the name Jug, and he wanted to torture Natalie until she gave up the pin numbers to their debit cards. The other man, named Peanut, wanted to take Natalie to the bank and force her to withdraw five-thousand dollars. The scrawny lady went by the name Tiny. Jug and Peanut asked for her opinion, but she did not care either way. Tiny was totally content with caring for Dominic.

Another storm cell brought back the heavy rain and ended the negotiations. Jug, Peanut, and Tiny continued to pass the whiskey bottle. The men drank until they passed out. Tiny passed out too, with Dominic protesting in her arms. Natalie stayed awake for most of the night. She finally drifted off after Dominic cried himself to sleep.

They woke up the next morning to Dominic's screaming. Tiny worked hard to soothe the baby while Jug and Peanut played rock-paper-scissors to determine their next move. Jug won and asked Natalie for the pin numbers to their debit cards. Natalie refused to talk. Peanut dangled a syringe in Natalie's face. He threatened to give Jermaine another injection and beating if she did not give up the pin numbers.

Natalie gave in and made a deal with the morons. She would give up the pin number to one debit card. She agreed to give up the remaining pin numbers if two conditions were met. First, she wanted to be untied and allowed to nurse her son. Secondly, she demanded something to eat for her and her husband. They agreed to her requests. Jug flashed one of the cards in front of her face and wrote the pin number in the palm of his hand.

The three morons came up with a plan of their own that required them to drive into town. Jug was to take the debit card and withdraw the daily limit from the it. Peanut was to buy beer, whiskey, and smokes. Tiny was to buy groceries. Tiny sat Dominic on top of her sleeping bag in the middle of the floor. The three morons left out together. This was a half hour before Lylah arrived.

* * *

Jermaine caught his breath when he made it to the truck, then he immediately went to work. He struggled immensely to free the tire, and he paused only for swift prayers and deep breaths. All four tires were back on the road after he sub-merged Dominic's car seat in the mud. He flipped the car seat over and used it as a ramp to steer the truck out of the sludge pit. Jermaine's brief victory gave way to another sudden concern. The truck was facing in the wrong direction. The risk of making a U-turn and getting stuck in the mud again proved too costly. Jermain put the truck in reverse and used his mirrors to drive backwards.

Dominic fell asleep in Natalie's arms. His eyes popped open a few times but only long enough to scan Natalie's face and doze back off. Lylah continued to rub her ankle even though it was numb. Lylah and Natalie comforted one another by re-stating the same phrase, "He'll make it in time."

They looked up when they heard the approaching vehicle. They got up and pushed their way through the woods and to the road. Jermaine drove past them but slammed on the brakes the moment he noticed them waving him down. He drove forward and made a hard left into the entrance of the drive-way followed by a quick back up and reverse. Jermaine parked the truck long enough to leap out and help Lylah into the back seat. Natalie jumped into the passenger seat with Dominic and fastened the seatbelt around them. Jermaine pressed hard on the gas pedal and fled the scene toward the main road.

Lylah spotted the red sedan through the back window. They were being chased. Jermaine was forced to reduce his speed when he made it to the last dangerous curve. His truck was faster than the sedan, but it also had a greater risk of toppling over. Jermaine patted the brakes and choked the stirring wheel until the road straightened out. There was a clear path to the stop sign at the main road, but the sedan was gaining speed.

Jermaine made a complete stop at the sign. Then he made a right turn onto the main road and floored the gas pedal again. The moron driving the sedan ignored the stop sign. He made a wide right turn and crashed into the police car that was heading in the opposite direction.

They all witnessed the collision, but no one spoke of it. The only sound inside the truck came from Dominic's soft snoring and the roaring engine. Jermaine merged onto the highway a half hour later.

* * *

Jermaine could no longer ignore the flashing fuel light. He pulled into the gas station at the halfway point. Lylah stared back at the people who gaped at her and Jermaine when they entered the gas station. Jermaine was shirtless and his upper body was littered with cuts and bruises. His once white J's were brown and unrecognizable. Jermaine held Lylah up as she hopped on one leg toward the restroom. Her clothes were caked with mud and gravel and so was the fabric tied around her ankle.

Natalie went inside the gas station when Lylah and Jermaine returned. Her nails were broken, her hair was a mess, and dried up tear marks covered her lower face. She returned to the truck with sandwiches and water. The food and drink made them perk up. There was a bit of small talk and then Jermaine turned the music on for the last part of the trip.

They made it back home at a quarter to nine. Jermaine parked the truck in front of the house and Lylah started laughing hysterically. Jermaine and Natalie looked at each other and then back at Lylah. She dried a small tear from her eye then announced, "I'm going to have an amazing freshman year!"

THE END

| 5 |

A DIFFERENT COLOR

D.L. glanced at the time on the bottom of his laptop. He turned it off and took off his suit jacket. He arranged it neatly on the back of his cozy chair and then he left the office. He poked his head into his supervisor's room and told her that he would be back after an extended lunch break. D.L. made another stop at the secretary's desk where he asked her to forward all his calls to voice mail. He left work behind and stepped out into the sunshine wearing his designer shades and his crisp white polo shirt.

He hopped in his new shiny black malibu, adjusted the mirrors, and pulled off. D.L. bobbed his head to the sounds that came from his speakers. He was confident about his new plan to straighten out Mike, his knuckle-headed younger brother. He turned the music down and cruised at a comfortable 15 miles per hour before parking in front of his old apartment building.

He pressed on the horn until Mike stuck his head out of the bedroom window. Mike yelled at D.L., "Come upstairs!" D.L. turned off the ignition, but he refused to get out the car.

From out of his driver's side mirror, D.L. saw his mother pull up in her silver cavalier. She parked two cars in back of him, and just like D.L., she just sat there. He could clearly see her but she could not see him.

D.L. sent a text to Mike, "*Let's go*." And then, out of curiosity, he sent one to his mother, *"Where are you?"*

His mother texted back first, "leaving *work*". Mike's reply came back a few minutes later and simply read, "*come up for a minute*". D.L. texted him back, "*u supposed to b ready; gotta go back to work soon, let's go!*"

D.L. looked at his mother through his rearview mirror. She sat with a tiresome look on her face and a lit cigarette perched in between her lips. D.L. wondered what was on her mind and why she sat outside her own apartment blowing cigarette smoke out the car window. As he wondered about her thoughts, D.L. began to question himself about how things ended up the way they were.

Ten years had passed since Mike was badly beaten at the neighborhood playground. His nose, jaw, and right leg were all broken. He had three cracked ribs and a punctured lung. It was a rough and painful recovery. D.L. blamed himself for glorifying the neighborhood set and for teaching Mike about the principles of ghetto life survival. Part of his teaching included how to remain fearless when confronted by an opp.

It was that fearlessness that led to Mike's beat down. As a result of his guilt, D.L. suffered from mild depression. Their mother, Ms. Jefferies, put the total blame for the incident on D.L. She rarely spoke to him, and the few times she did, she called him every name beneath a child of God.

D.L. continued to stare through his rearview mirror at his mother. She was on her second cigarette and her seat was slightly reclined. D.L. allowed his mind to slip back into the past again.

Mike slowly recovered from his wounds and so did the family. D.L. and Mike's street-life survival sessions were replaced with video game battles and biddy basketball tournaments. Ms. Jefferies started talking to D.L. again and things were alright. D.L. went off to college a few years later.

While in school, D.L. fell in love with his independence. Though the university was less than 100 miles away, he stayed away from home his entire freshman year. He came back after the spring semester of his sophomore year, and that is when he noticed a slight change in the family dynamics. Mike was only 12 but would leave at all times of the day and night and come in the house whenever he pleased. D.L. continued his seasonal visits home and every time it was another transfer of power from his mama to Mike.

"That boy gonna do what he gonna do," was Ms. Jefferies answer whenever D.L. addressed the subject of Mike. After graduation, D.L. moved back to the city and found a job and a place of his own. He stopped addressing the subject of Mike altogether.

Twenty minutes had passed since he pulled up to the apartment, and D.L. watched his mother light up a third cigarette. He could not see his mother's tears, but he could tell they were there. D.L. opened his door, and a sudden knock on the passenger's side window made him jump.

"Look at this dude," laughed Mike. He was talking to the three guys who came out the apartment building with him. They were all older and a lot bigger than Mike.

"I'll holla at y'all later. And Big Tim, hop on your bike and handle that for me," Mike said to the heavyset man in diamond earrings and thick chain.

Mike jumped in on the passenger's side. He closed the door and looked over at D.L., "Quit being so jumpy, D. Ain't nobody gonna mess with you over here."

"I ain't jumpy," D.L. objected. He starting the car then continued, "I just don't like coming around here." D.L. took one last look at their mother through his rearview mirror.

"This where you grew up, D. What you mean you don't like it over here?" Mike turned the music up and didn't wait for a response. "Let's get this over with, big bruh."

D.L. pulled off and circled the block. "What you doing?" asked Mike.

"I'm about to say hi to Mama."

"She ain't at home."

D.L. pulled up to the front of the apartment building as Ms. Jeffries was walking up the sidewalk. Mike rolled down his window, "What's up, Ma."

Surprise painted her face. She gave a half wave and then quickened her pace toward the door. D.L. got out the car and called out, "You got a minute Mama?"

"I'm waiting on a phone call," she responded without looking back.

D.L. got back in the car and drove off. He wondered out loud, "What was that all about?"

"Mama does her own thing, man," answered Mike. "I be about my business, and she be about hers."

* * *

She must have repeated the same line a million times before. Her manner was firm and serious though she stood no more than five feet tall. "Have ready the full name and the doc number of the person you're visiting!" The creases in her uniform were perfect, and like a drill sergeant, her eyes paced back and forth at the people waiting in line.

"Henry J. Walker," D.L. responded when it was his turn to sign in. The officer looked through the binder full of papers and checked off D.L.'s name. Mike's name was not on the visitors' list, but all was cleared after a quick phone call. D.L. and Mike were directed to the waiting room.

When their names were called, D.L. and Mike put their jewelry and phones in a locker and passed through the metal detectors. They were escorted to the visiting room where the inmates were allowed to sit with their guests. Hank was already in the room. When he saw D.L. and Mike he stood up in his orange jump suit and yelled out to them, "What y'all got on my snacks?!"

D.L. bought his old friend Hank a bag of chips and a cola from out the vending machines. Hank greeted them with a handshake hug combination, and they all sat down for conversation. It took Mike a while to relax. While Hank and D.L. talked about the good old days, Mike observed his surroundings.

First, he looked around at the other inmates and their guests. Then he counted the number of vending machines against the back wall and the security cameras hanging from the ceiling. After he met eyes with the officer who stood by the entrance, Mike turned back around to join Hank and D.L.

"Alright little brother," D.L. patted Mike on the back. "You know why I brought you here. I'm gonna' get a bag of chips while you sit and listen to what my buddy Hank has to say." D.L. left the table.

Like a sermon at church, Hank did all the talking, and Mike was a one-man congregation. He sat there shaking his head and playing with his fingers. Hank continued to grill Mike while D.L. threw back Doritos and traced his thoughts back to the past.

After Mike got out the hospital D.L. and Hank promised to get revenge on whoever was accountable. The word on the street was that Marvin, a neighborhood thug seeking to build a reputation, was responsible for what happened to Mike. D.L. and Hank kept quiet about their plan while finding out as much as they could about Marvin. Although he attended a high school across town, they found out where he lived and who he hung out with.

They followed Marvin to a birthday party one night over winter break and waited for him outside in the alley. On his way home, D.L. and Hank appeared from behind the dumpster and attacked him. They gave him an old fashion beat down. Hank did not want to stop, but D.L. pulled him off after he estimated Marvin's injuries to be slightly more than those inflicted on Mike.

The first school day after winter break, was when D.L. found out that Marvin had been killed. D.L. and Hank were talking about it on their way home from school. D.L. was joking when he asked Hank if he was the one who did it. But he never did forget the fiendish look in Hank's eyes when he looked up and replied, "Would you blame me if I did?"

D.L. and Hank's friendship dwindled during their second year in high school. Hank started getting in trouble more frequently and was bounced back and forth between his mother and his father who lived in Minneapolis.

For every year D.L. spent in college Hank did half a year in jail. It started with possession of a firearm. Then it was drug possession with a firearm. Finally, the charge was attempted murder in which Hank unsuccessfully claimed self-defense.

"So, what I'm saying to you is funny?!" Hank kicked the chair Mike was sitting in.

"Not really," Mike gave a half laugh. "You've got your take on things, and I got mine."

"Same thing I use to say on the other side of these walls!"

"Look, whateva man." Mike looked over at D.L. and stood up, "It's time to go!"

Hank stood up too and got in Mike's face, "So what I gotta say ain't important, lil' Mikey?!"

"It's like I said, whateva!"

The tension between the two was enough to rouse the guards' attention, and they quickly moved toward the confrontation. Two officers attempted to escort Hank back to his cell, but he was not making it easy for them. He tried to break free from their hold to get at Mike.

"My fault, Hank," yelled D.L. "I thought you could get through to him, but I guess he's gotta learn on his own!" Hank looked back over his shoulder and replied, "You right, D.L., but don't worry. I'll look out for him when he ends up in here with me!"

The ride back to the city was quiet. D.L. and Mike were both defeated. D.L.'s desperate attempt to reach his little brother failed, and Mike was not going to get back the last two hours of his life.

* * *

A full week had passed since D.L.'s failed attempt at a scared straight intervention for Mike. D.L. had not heard from Mike or his mother until his phone started to vibrate in the middle of his afternoon meeting at work. D.L. kept blocking his mother's repeated calls until the meeting was over. On the way back to his office he walked by his secretary, and she handed him a yellow sticky note that simply read:

3:10 P.M. Call your mother ASAP!

D.L. closed the door behind him, sat in his chair, and started to reflect. D.L.'s office was a miniature version of the United Center. He had Chicago Bulls memorabilia everywhere: trash can, wall clock, posters, paper weight, and even an area rug. He grabbed the mini basketball from off his desk and shot it across the room and into the netted rim. The ball traveled through a long plastic tube that led back to his desk.

D.L. took a deep breath and then pressed the answer button on his phone when the picture of his mother made the screen glow again. Thirty minutes after taking his mother's call, D.L. pulled up to an open spot four blocks away from her apartment. He finished off the last sip of his coffee and observed the scene before him.

He stepped out the car with anchors on his feet. Whatever crime that had been committed behind the yellow tape, occurred in daylight and drew the attention of dozens of bystanders. D.L. forced his way closer for a better view. His phone started humming, and he answered it without looking at the screen, "I'm here, Mama. Trying to see what's up. Gotta go."

Like a studio audience, the ever-growing crowd had a clear view of the happenings beyond the blockade, and like a potato chip on an anthill, the scene was full of activity. There were several officers in uniform and some in plain clothes, all conversing amongst themselves. They were master surgeons paying close attention to every aspect of the landscape. There were orange cones, police cruisers, an ambulance, and even a news reporter with her cameraman.

There was a motorcycle flipped on its side, and next to it were two black body bags. D.L. stood close to the action with a few other people, and all were mentally repeating the same five words, *please don't let it be.*

While D.L. patrolled the crime scene, Ms. Jefferies paced the width of her living room floor with her phone in one hand and a cigarette in the other. She often stopped pacing long enough to glance at her phone or to look out the living room window onto the street below. She made a detour to the kitchen table where the make-do ashtray, an aluminum can, caught the wormlike string of ash from her cigarette. She was already on her third one.

She lit the first cigarette a couple hours back when she made it home from work and pulled into her parking space. She rolled the window down, reclined in her seat, and stayed put until Mike left the apartment. On her way into the house, she walked past Mike, and with barely a "hey mama", he hopped on the back of his Big Tim's motorcycle, and they sped off.

She made it into the apartment and put the pack of smokes back in her purse. She tossed her purse on the coffee table only to reverse her actions a short time later after she heard the gun shots. She lit the second cigarette and dropped it from her lips when she heard the words of someone on the street below. It was not the tone of the words but what was actually said that forced Ms. Jefferies to clutch her stomach.

"I think Mike just got hit! Go and tell his mama!"

The banging on the door started, but Ms. Jefferies ignored it. She picked up the cigarette, stomped out the embers, and grabbed her phone. She kept trying to reach D.L. at work, but he was not answering.

When D.L. finally answered his phone, Ms. Jefferies told him about the gunshots and what she heard about Mike. After she ended the call, she started to pace back and forth. She lit up the third cigarette when D.L. made it to the scene of the shooting.

A loud and sudden knock rattled the door a few minutes later and caused Ms. Jefferies' heart to skip a beat. She opened the door for D.L., and even though he entered the house with soothing news, she wore an uneasy grin on her face.

"I can't take it anymore!" She finally stopped pacing. "I'm glad that wasn't Mikey, but I'm sick of wondering when and if something bad is going to happen to him."

"I know, mama. You should be fed up. You didn't let me get away with half the crap Mikey gets away with. The boy is out of control." Ms. Jeffries shot D.L. an evil gaze. If looks could cut, D.L. would have received a thick slash across his forehead. But still he continued, "I know you don't want to hear it, but you spoiled him. And now like I said, the boy is OC."

She tried to hold back the tears, but D.L. had already turned on the faucet. Ms. Jeffries stood to her feet and cried, "I did my best! You think it was easy for me to raise y'all by myself?!" She didn't wait for his reply, "It wasn't, Darius!"

Like two heavyweight boxers at the end of a round, D.L. and his mother went to their separate corners. Ms. Jefferies sat on the loveseat, and D.L. sat in a folding chair close to the living room window. Facing each other, they sat in harmony, but the silence continued even after D.L. got up. He kissed his mother on the cheek and left the apartment.

* * *

It wasn't too unusual for D.L. to put in overtime on a Friday evening, especially after a super busy week. On this particular Friday evening, he completed the paperwork for his existing cases and organized the files of six new ones. He then took notes on the 15 voice messages left on his work phone. His finally called it quits after responding to several e-mails.

Before locking up the office, D.L. set his briefcase by the door and gripped the mini basketball in the palm of his hand. A made basket all the way from the office door usually meant a good weekend was in store for him. The ball traveled straight toward the basket, made contact with the thick plastic rim, and slowly circled around it. The ball came to a complete stop. It did not drop in the net, nor did it fall to the ground. It just stayed there.

With the music blasting, D.L. drove through the downtown streets with his windows down. He was caught by the streetlight in front of his favorite nightlife spot. He heard the joyous sounds and watched as the happy people celebrated Friday night under the canopy. D.L. spotted several casual associates, yet he resisted the urge to join them. He let out a mighty yawn and when the light turned green, he put his foot on the gas pedal and headed for home.

D.L. pulled into his parking space at the rear entrance of his apartment, grabbed his briefcase from out the backseat, and locked the door behind him. He lived on the second floor of a spacious building fifteen minutes north of downtown. It was one of four small brick buildings owned by the same company. All four units formed a semi-circle facing a duck pond.

After climbing up the stairs to his front door, D.L. came to an abrupt halt as he heard noise coming from inside his apartment. He took out his phone and crept closer toward the door. There was loud talking and laughter. D.L. put the phone back in his pocket and charged toward the door. He put the key in, turned the knob, and flung the door open.

"How did you get in here, Mikey?!" D.L. was heated.

"Hello big brother! Nice to see you too!"

D.L.'s temper was raging as he glanced around. There were opened cans and potato chip bags scattered around his kitchen and living room, and weed smoke filled the air. Mike and Big Tim were sitting at the dining room table with a girl he'd never seen before. Seated comfortably on D.L.'s black leather couch, was two of Mike's other friends. They were watching a moving on D.L.'s big screen TV, and the sound competed with the music that was coming from Mike's phone.

The random voices and the mixture of noise was enough to make D.L. snap off, "Get out!" His tone was forceful and enough to stop all conversations. But even though D.L. stood holding his door wide open, the uninvited visitors were hesitant to leave.

"Y'all must need some encouragement, huh?" D.L. laughed and then he gave them a warning, "Be here when I get back."

He disappeared into the back room, and all eyes turned to Mike. He shrugged his shoulders and gave a simple suggestion, "Y'all betta bounce." His company made a quick exit. Mike turned off the music and the TV, and then he started to clean up the bottles and chip bags. He braced himself for a showdown with D.L.

With an aluminum bat in his hand, D.L. charged from the back room. He looked around then bolted straight up to Mike and pointed the tip of the bat in Mike's face. "How did you get in here?!"

Mike pushed the bat away, but D.L. gripped it with both hands and held it to Mike's neck. He pushed him against the wall with it. Mike tried to free himself, but he could not. He submitted and stared into the furious eyes of his bigger and much stronger brother. "I'll ask you again, Mikey, how did you get into my apartment?" Angry sprinkles of spit shot out of D.L.'s mouth and into Mike's face.

Mike struggled to answer, "I can't breathe."

D.L. took some of his weight off the bat. "You didn't lock the deadbolt," Mike managed to speak, "and I was able to pick the bottom lock."

"Why you always got to mess things up, Mikey?!"

"Nobody even saw me," pleaded Mike.

D.L. abandoned his hold on Mike and put the bat down to his side. With his free hand he gave Mike a violent push. Mike fell and slid across the laminated floor. D.L. stood above him and stared. Mike used his forearm as a shield, but the assault was over.

"Get out Mikey!" demanded D.L.

"Hold up!" Mike shot to his feet and galloped to the other side of the table and out of D.L.'s striking range. "I can't leave, D.L., ain't got no place to go!"

At a walking pace, D.L. began to chase Mike around the dining room table. "That's not my concern, Mikey, and neither are you."

"Just because you got a nice job and this upscale apartment, you think you too good for me now, bruh?"

"What?!" D.L.'s face turned even angrier and the chase around the table went from slow speed to a faster pace.

"I take that back," declared Mike. "That sounded stupid, and I know it. And that was even more stupid of me to invite my people over to chill at your fancy spot. For some reason Mama started tripping and she kicked me out. Can you believe that? Anyway, I just needed somebody to talk to. And that somebody turned into some bodies. And then I got hungry so I had my home girl hook up some spaghetti. And it just took off from there."

Mike made a bold move. He stopped moving when he was at the head of the table and the furthest away from the door.

He looked up at D.L. and asked, "Do you remember what you told me when I came home from the hospital after Marvin and his boys beat the crap out of me?" D.L. did not answer, and he gave up on chasing Mike around the table.

"You told me that you would always have my back. Now I really need you to hold true to your words. I'm not trying to sleep in the streets, bruh. I just need some time to get myself together until mama stops tripping."

D.L.'s thoughts took him back to that moment at the community center when he first heard that something bad had happened to Mike. In a game of twenty-one, D.L. held the lead with 18 points. He shot a three-point basket and netted it for the game. D.L. and Hank were walking toward the water fountain when Herb ran into the gym and yelled out, "D.L.! Mike just got mobbed on! Hurry up!"

D.L. refused to think about the details that followed. Instead, he pointed the bat at Mike, "You got one month, Mikey! That's enough time for you to get your act together and to fix things with mama. And I got a bunch of rules and regulations to hit you with. First, I'm gonna hit up this shower."

The steaming shower dropped miniature missiles all over D.L.'s body. The hot water was enough to relax, but the situation with Mike was still top priority. D.L. put on his spider man boxers and a fresh white tee. He joined Mike in the living room. D.L. grabbed the remote, flopped down in his chair, turned the TV off, and jumped right into it.

"Rule number one, respect my spot." D.L. pointed at the coffee table. It was made of stained glass and bronze trimming. "You can start by cleaning away those water rings that your people left on my glass table.

"Rule number two, respect my private space and my stuff. There is no reason for you to ever go into my bedroom. And this beautiful black suede lazy-boy that I'm sitting in is only for me." D.L. stared into Mike's eyes, "Don't ever sit in this chair, Mikey.

"Rule number three, clean up behind yourself. And I don't like the smell of piss so watch your aim in the bathroom.

"Rule number four, man up. This means when I'm not at home, neither are you."

"But where am I supposed to go?!" Mike protested.

"Until you get a job, you should be out looking for one, or at the library, or in somebody's school. You get where I'm going with this, Mikey? You should be doing something productive, something that's gonna help you out in your current situation. And if I were you, I wouldn't wait too long to find a job."

To make his point, D.L. walked to the kitchen and pointed to the calendar that was pinned to the wall. "You owe me $485 on rent, and it's due at the end of your thirty days. Any more questions Mikey?"

Mike shook his head. "Nope. That sounds easy enough."

They sat in silence for a few moments. Mike processed the rules he had been given, and D.L. checked to see if he needed to add on to the list. Mike broke the silence moments later when he pointed toward the hallway, "Go and get it!"

"What you talking about, Mikey?"

"The old PS. I know you still got it! Remember that basketball game we used to play?"

"Live?"

"Yep, that's the one!"

"I don't play video games no more, Mikey."

"That's right, I forgot who I was talking to," teased Mike. "You ain't D.L. anymore! You're Mr. Serious now, with the fancy car, the fancy job, the fancy apartment, and the fancy briefcase. And you don't have time to play unfancy games with your little brother."

D.L. left the comfort of his chair and walked away.

"You don't have to leave Mr. Serious!" Mike shouted behind him. "I won't talk about your fancy table, or your fancy chair, or your fancy floors, or your fancy curtains, or your fancy bat, or your fancy toilet."

D.L. returned a short while later with the PS. He connected it to the big screen and threw one of the controllers to Mike.

"Mr. Serious is about to give his little brother a serious beat down on his fancy TV with his old but fancy game system."

* * *

D.L. stood at his office door with a good grip around the mini basketball. With perfect posture he flicked his wrist and released the ball from his hand. The ball sailed through the air with an awesome arch and dropped flawlessly through the net. D.L. grabbed his briefcase and locked the door behind him. He left the office a lot sooner than he had the Friday before.

He was forced to maneuver through the evening rush. Traffic was bumper to bumper, and it was every driver's desire to make it home and leave work behind for a couple of days. D.L. got caught again by the streetlight in front of his favorite nightlife spot. He rolled his window down and switched from the radio to his favorite weekend mix. D.L watched as the workers prepared for the future Friday crowd by setting up the outside patio and sound stage. D.L. whispered, *see you soon* and then he pulled off when the light turned green.

When D.L. turned off the main street into his apartment complex, he saw Mike's friend, Big Tim. They made eye contact and Big Tim gave D.L. a nod. Big Tim pulled out his phone and started texting. D.L. kept his gaze on Big Tim until he turned into the back parking lot. Mike was sitting on the ground next to the apartment door when D.L. made it up the stairs.

"It's about time you made it home," announced Mike.

D.L. stuck the key in the keyhole and then looked over at Mike, "I need to holla at you."

"Can it wait, D.L.? I gotta get in and get out. I got something to do."

D.L. opened the door and walked in. "All I need is a minute."

After a quick trip to the bathroom, D.L. joined Mike in the living room. He sat in his black suede chair and shook his head in disapproval. "It's only been a week and you already messed up, Mikey!"

"Don't come at me like that, D.L. I'm not six. If you got something to say, speak up, bruh."

"Alright, cool," D.L. replied. He sat at the edge of his chair and continued, "You broke all the rules, little brother, so you gotta go. I tried to help you, but it's not working out."

Mike's mouth popped open like a small child on Christmas morning. "That's a lie, D.L.! Which one of your rules did I break?!" Mike sat on the edge of the couch and gave D.L. his full attention.

"Rule number four, when I'm not at home, neither are you. I know you were just in here because you left the light on in the bathroom. I turned off all the lights before I left this morning. And plus, Mikey, you haven't been looking for work. I haven't seen any job applications around here.

"And then there's rule number one, respect my spot. You got Big Tim walking around the front of my building like he's guarding something. And I know he tipped you off that I was on my way up. What you gotta say now, Mikey?"

Mike stood to his feet. "Where am I supposed to go, Darius?"

"I don't know, Mikey. You call yourself a man. Now you gotta think like one."

"So that's it, huh?" Mike's eyes were full of water, but he did not shed a tear. "I'm a hustler because of you, and now you wanna bail on me because you caught a lucky break?"

D.L. stood to his feet, "What are you talking about, Mikey?"

"I'm talking about you, D.L.! You taught me about the streets and the hustlin'."

"Yeah, I did! And then I took it back after you got mobbed on. Remember? I made things right, Mikey. I changed. I graduated from high school and from college. You were supposed to be watching me!"

"How was I supposed to be watching you and surviving at the same time?!"

Mike reached in his front pocket and pulled out a wad of cash. "It's not about red. It's not about blue. It's about a different color. You see this green?" Mike held the wad of cash up for D.L. to see. "I didn't finish high school, and I'm a long way from college, but I know how to make this fast green. So, I guess I don't need you after all, D.L."

Mike counted and separated half the rent money from his stash and threw it on D.L.'s glass table. Then he left the apartment without speaking another word.

D.L. stared at the cash. He tossed it into one of the kitchen drawers on his way to the back room. D.L. took out his clippers for a quick lining and then he stepped into the shower. He got dressed in a new outfit and pulled out the matching shoes. He secured the quarter-karat earring in his ear and fastened the two-tone Movado watch to his wrist. D.L. grabbed his keys and locked the door behind him.

With the weekend mix pouring out of his speakers, D.L. rolled the front windows down and headed toward his favorite hangout spot with the lights of the city illuminating the way.

* * *

D.L. had deep fried shrimp, French fries, a side salad, and an orange soda for lunch. He ate alone in the parking lot of the Shrimp House while preparing for his second home visit. It was 12:30 in the afternoon and D.L. had already attended one home visit and appeared at two court hearings. After the heavy lunch, D.L. put the coordinates in his phone's GPS and headed to the other side of the city.

Before getting out the car, D.L. took a long look around the outside of the house, something he did before every home visit. He was there to visit Roxie and her four-year-old son, Corey. On the way up the sidewalk, D.L. mentally reviewed the details of Roxie's case.

Roxie Roberson was a 26-year-old recovering meth addict. Roxie and her son entered the system two years ago after an anonymous call lead police and CPS to her one-bedroom apartment on the south side of the city. It was in the middle of winter. They found the toddler alone in the cluttered apartment. The floor was covered with trash and clothes. Two-year-old Corey stood in the center of the living room with tears on his grimy face and an overfilled diaper sagging from his skinny body. Tightly clutched in his little hands was a sippy cup full of clotted milk.

Roxie made it back just in time to watch as her child, cradled in a thick blanket, was carried away to an unfamiliar car. Enraged, Roxie went off on everybody. The drama escalated when one of the officers read Roxie her rights and attempted to handcuff her. She went off again. Only this time she used her fists, teeth, and feet. It took three officers to handcuff Roxie and get her in the back of the squad car. The events of that night ended her 72-hour drug binge.

Roxie met D.L. at the door and then offered him a seat on the couch. She was short, well mannered, nicely dressed, and soft spoken. D.L. gave a proper introduction to Roxie and Corey who was playing with his toy truck on the living room floor. D.L. took the tablet out of his briefcase and began asking

Roxie questions. Though the questions were mandatory, D.L. relied mostly on what he was able to observe during the tour.

Roxie's house was nothing like her former apartment, the one described in the report. This house was small, both inside and out, but everything was in its place. Every room was neat and clean. D.L. was satisfied with Roxie's progress and found it hard to believe that this was the same person in the report.

After the tour Roxie and D.L. sat on the couch for a second round of questions. He asked about any temptations of drug use, her employment status, and plans for Corey's education. He rarely looked up from his notes as he grilled Roxie on her new lifestyle. Roxie's transformation from the time of her arrest to the present was startling but in a good way.

When D.L. got up to leave, Corey told him a knock-knock joke, and they all laughed hard. When Roxie laughed, she revealed an omen from her old life, meth mouth. Roxie had a hole in her front tooth and the other one was showing signs of decay.

After the visit, D.L. got back in his car and pulled off. Without planning to do so, he drove from Roxie's house to his mother's apartment. Cruising at a comfortable 15 MPH, D.L. patrolled with his windows down. Before he made it to the apartment building, D.L. noticed that the window in his mother's apartment was slightly open. He concluded that his mother gave in and that Mike was living back at home with her.

No sooner than he drove past the building, D.L. spotted Mike. He stood outside leaning against a light pole. He was hanging with some of the same friends that was in D.L.'s apartment three and a half weeks back. Mike met eyes with D.L. and the staring battle began. It was cold and intense. No form of communication was exchanged, not even a simple head nod.

D.L. continued the stare down for as long as he could. He turned back toward the steering wheel just in time. He miscalculated his timing and slammed on the brakes a few feet after the stop sign. He almost hit a pedestrian who was walking across the street.

The man crossing the street quickly glanced in D.L.'s direction, "Be more careful, little brother!"

"Who you calling little brother?" D.L. teased. "We the same age!"

"D.L.? Is that you?!" the pedestrian exclaimed.

"Yep, it's me! Get in the car, O'Shea!"

D.L. and O'Shea went to school together, elementary and middle school. They went to different high schools, but they always kept in contact until recent years.

O'Shea was a big guy with an even bigger voice. He stood over six feet tall and was built like a defensive football player. He walked over to the passenger's side and got in the car. He adjusted the seat to his comfort.

"Where are you headed, O'Shea?"

"You can take me home, D.L."

D.L. pulled off, and then he asked, "Where you coming from?"

"Bible study. Then I stopped by your mother's crib. Tried to talk some sense into your little brother and his friends."

"Good luck with that! I tried to help Mikey, but he wasn't feeling me."

"I was getting to him, I can tell," O'Shea replied. "He tried to play it off since he was around his people, but I opened his eyes a little, and I'm gonna keep on him too! When these young dudes see me coming, they want to run. But unlike the police, they can't run from me, because they know I can find em'."

O'Shea slapped his heavy hand on his lap and laughed. His laugh was deep, long, loud, and contagious. It made D.L. laugh.

"I see you ain't changed a bit, O'Shea. You are a true urban missionary! This hood is blessed to have you, dude. For real."

O'Shea suddenly turned serious.

"I'm not doing anything special, D.L. These young dudes need somebody to tell them the truth, and that's what the Holy Spirit sent me to do."

D.L. parked in front of O'Shea's house and turned off the ignition. Their conversation went from the hood to middle school house parties and then back to the neighborhood. When O'Shea started talking about Mike again and his connection to Hank, D.L. grew quiet. He just listened.

O'Shea continued, "I tried to tell Mike a long time ago that once he started working for Hank, it was gonna be hard to separate from him. Hank might be behind bars, but he still running thangs."

D.L. sat with his fists clutched. He felt sick, but he did not show any signs of it. "O'Shea, how long has Mikey been working for Hank?"

"You didn't know, D.L.?!"

"I didn't, but I do now." D.L.'s voice was calm, contrary to the surprise and anger that was brewing inside him.

"Mike said that you knew about it, but that you didn't care. I should've known that was big a lie."

"Lying. That's one of Mikey's strengths." D.L. started the car. "It was nice kicking it with you, O'Shea, but I gotta go."

"You good, D.L.?"

"Yep, I'm good."

O'Shea got out the car, and then they exchanged numbers. "Lock me in, D.L., and let's keep in touch." O'Shea tapped on the hood of D.L.'s car, and then he walked into the house after D.L. sped away.

D.L. looked at the time on his phone. It was a quarter after three. He called his secretary and told her that he would not be returning to the office. After he hung up with her, he turned off his phone. Instead of taking the highway toward his apartment, D.L. joined the east bound traffic and headed straight toward the prison.

* * *

D.L. walked into the public entrance at 4:00. When he stepped up to the sign-in desk, everything became quiet, and all eyes were on him. The lady at the desk looked at the clock on the wall. Then she greeted D.L., "It's a little late in the day, baby."

"Visiting hours still over at five?" he asked.

"That's right."

"Then I'm good." He slapped his driver's license on the desk in front of her. "I'm here to see Henry J. Walker."

She paused for a few seconds, rolled her eyes, and then took his license. She quickly typed the information in her computer and then she directed him to the empty waiting room. The security officers outside the waiting room were in rare form. They were laughing and joking around. Even the short lady from his previous visit was in a good mood. She no longer had the swag of a military officer.

D.L. sat alone in the waiting room ignoring the joyful workers as they celebrated their last hour on the job. As the clock inched closer to 5:00, the happy noises elevated and so did D.L.'s anger for Hank. D.L. made an attempt to block out the cheerful chatter by focusing on what he planned to say to Hank. He was riled up.

D.L. was eventually escorted to the visitation room at 4:30 sharp. The room was empty, except for a businessman in a suit sitting across the table from one of the incarcerated inmates. There was also an older couple visiting a younger inmate. One of the guards briefly made eye contact with D.L., glanced down at his watch, then continued his post at the front of the room.

Hank was escorted through the door a few minutes later. "What you got on my snacks, D.L.?!" Hank yelled from across the room with a wide smile on his face.

D.L.'s response came after Hank was seated. "Ain't here to talk about snacks, Hank. You owe me an explanation." His tone was even.

Hank's smile quickly evaporated. "An explanation?" A half smirk appeared on his face. "Explain to me, D.L., how I owe you an explanation?" Hank's voice was steady and calm.

"I'm talking about Mikey, Hank!" D.L.'s voice was less calm and grew impatient. "Why am I hearing from the streets that you got my little brother hustling for you? I even brought him up here so that you could point him in the right direction, but you played me!"

"I'm gonna hit you with two things, D.L. Then I'm going back to my cell so listen carefully." Hank's voice remained steady. With each syllable he spoke, Hank pounded his right fist into the open palm of his left hand. "Thing number one, the streets talk too much." When Hank stood up, he caught the guard's attention. "Thing number two, the activity between me and my business partner is not of your concern." The guard muttered something into his radio.

D.L. stood to his feet quicker than a toaster can throw up a pop tart. He took a step closer to Hank. "As of today, it's over Hank! Mikey ain't your pigeon anymore!"

Hank took a step closer to D.L. "Now you know that ain't up to you! Face it, D.L., I'm more of a big brother to Mikey than you ever were!"

D.L. pushed Hank and Hank tackled D.L. They both fell to the ground and then the punches started to fly. It took only seconds for the visitation room to flood with officers. Like conjoined twins, D.L. and Hank were physically separated, but the war of words grew stronger.

It took several officers to restrain Hank. His muscular body made the process of dragging him to the door very difficult. In the battle of words, Hank's voice was no longer steady and calm, instead he spat venom. "You didn't raise him right D.L.! But he knows who his real brother is!"

One of the officers secured D.L., but he could not stop him from arguing with Hank. "Whateva, Hank! Mikey's dead to you now! Find another goon!"

Though the officers were pulling hard, Hank grabbed on to the edge of the wall. He held on long enough to yell his last words across the room at D.L., "Can you put money in his pockets, D.L.?! Can you protect him from those headhunters on the street, D.L.?! No, you can't! But I can!" The officers were finally able to peel Hank away from the door and out of the visitation room.

Once the doors were closed, Hank stopped tussling. He was still able to see D.L. through the transparent windows while being escorted down the corridor.

D.L. held his gaze on Hank as well. Though Hank could no longer hear him, D.L. claimed the last words of the heated scuffle, "Mikey don't need you, Hank! He's gonna get it right."

Once Hank was out of view, D.L. looked around the room. During the conflict, the other two inmates had been escorted out of the visitation room, but the three visitors remained. They were huddled in one corner of the room. Their eyes locked on D.L.

"I'm sorry we messed up y'all's visit," he apologized. "I'm just trying to look out for my little brother, that's all."

* * *

The drive back to the city was a lot less stressful than the drive to the prison. Rush hour traffic died down and the highway lanes were wide open. D.L. got off on the exit closest to his mother's house with a sense of urgency. He was on a mission to find Mike and end his business venture with Hank.

D.L. pulled up to a different scene altogether. He parked behind his mother's car and looked around. There was no sign of Mike or anyone else. The block was still and oddly quiet. Not even a street cat or an anxious squirrel could be spotted.

D.L. let himself into his mother's apartment. First, he searched the kitchen, and then he popped his head into all the other rooms. He walked back to the living room and met his mother's cold stare. "Why you searching my house like you the police, D.L.?"

"Sorry mama." He kissed her on the cheek. "I'm looking for Mikey. Where is he?"

"He left about an hour ago."

"Did he say where he was going?"

"No, and I didn't ask!"

"You need to keep a tab on him, Mama."

"Don't start with me, D.L.!"

"I'm just saying, he's up to no good in these streets."

"Look! I care about Mikey, and I worry about him, that's why I let him move back in. At least I know where he is after dark. I tried talking sense into him. I tried to get him back in school. I even had a job lined up for him, but he refused to show up. Mikey is going make his own choices and mistakes. I can only pray for him and put it in God's hands."

D.L. flopped down on the couch. Ms. Jefferies continued to talk, but D.L. tuned her out. His thoughts shifted back to his visit with Hank. He recalled the furious look on Hank's face when he told him that Mikey was no longer his pigeon. His thoughts then shifted to the night he'd kicked Mikey out of his apartment. He visualized the hunger in Mike's eyes when he lifted up the wad of cash and declared, *"But I know how to make this fast green."*

D.L.'s thoughts shifted one final time. He recalled the lady in the flower print dress that he stood next to at the crime scene a few weeks earlier. He stood with her and a few other people, waiting for the identification of the two dead bodies. In slow-motion, the reporting officer stepped under the yellow tape and walked up to the lady. He spoke a few simple words to her, and she fell to her knees and let out a soul-piercing scream.

D.L. snapped out of the flashbacks and stood to his feet. Ms. Jefferies was still talking, when he interrupted her by kissing her on the cheek. "I gotta go find Mikey, Mama. He might be in trouble."

"What makes you say that D.L.?"

"I just got a feeling, that's all. I'll call you if I hear from him, and you do the same."

D.L. drove the streets of the neighborhood, but he was not able to find Mike. He asked a few familiar faces about Mike's

location but to no benefit. After an hour and a half of searching, D.L. gave his mother a follow up call and then drove to
his Northside apartment. After a frozen dinner of meatloaf
and potatoes, D.L. watched the sports network until he fell
asleep in his black suede chair.

* * *

D.L. stubbed his big toe against the coffee table and knocked
his knee against the bar stool on his way to the peephole. The
sound of a desperate fist hitting the door combined with the
noise of the brass knocker, gave D.L. an instant headache. He
peeked through the peephole then unlocked the door. D.L. let
out a big yawn before he greeted Mike, "I've been looking for
you all evening, and of course you show up after midnight."

D.L. moved to the side. Mike walked straight into the
living room with D.L. on his heels. With a blank look on his
face, he flopped down on the couch, grabbed a throw pillow,
and threw it across the room.

"Let me guess," started D.L. He sat in his recliner and
leaned back. "You're in trouble, aren't you?"

Mike let out a big sigh before answering. "Yeah. You can
say that."

D.L. spoke again after two minutes of silence. "Well, that
dumb look on your face is not giving me much to go by, so I
guess you need to start talking."

"Be patient with me, D.L." Mike paused before he continued, "I'm having a hard time processing what just happened."

There was another long moment of silence, and D.L. broke it again. "Tell you what, Mikey. Hit me up tomorrow. I'm too tired for this tonight." D.L. stood to his feet.

Mike opened his mouth. "I don't know if he's alive or if he's dead. But O'Shea got shot," he let out an even longer sigh, "and I was right there, D.L."

"What?!" D.L. sat back down in his chair. Only this time he did not recline. He sat straight up and looked his brother in the face. D.L. carefully played each scene in his mind, as Mike recounted the events from the last several hours.

"I saw you drive by the apartment earlier today. And I know you saw me. I was even watching when you almost hit O'Shea. Then you gave him a ride. Nothing much was happening on the block so me and my people went our separate ways.

"Mama came home with some burgers. I was in my phone and eating my food at the same time. It was after five when Big Tim sent me a text to meet him at his mama's house. That's usually where we meet up and discuss our orders from Hank. Yeah, you heard me. I work for Hank, but that's a whole different story that we can get into later. Anyway, I met up with Big Tim around10 o'clock.

"Hank's orders are usually the same. Pick this package up from here and take it over there. Split this package up. Collect the cash. Count out your portion and stash the rest. Stuff like that. But this time it was different. Hank wanted me and Big Tim to go check somebody. This somebody apparently had his nose in Hank's business. Hank has other people for stuff like that, but I messed up and went along anyway."

Mike took a deep breath. "The mission was supposed to be simple. My job was to stay in the background at the gas station and make sure nobody was watching while Big Tim showed off his gun and told this somebody to stay out of Hank's business. Big Tim called it a scare tactic.

"There were three older dudes in front of the gas station when we made it there. They were standing around and talking. As we got closer, I recognized O'Shea by his loud laugh. I didn't know the other two guys. One of the dudes got on his bike and rolled off first. Then the older cat drove off in a black truck.

"I thought the mission was over after they left, but Big Tim kept walking toward the gas station and towards O'Shea. It felt like someone kicked me in the face when Big Tim pointed to O'Shea and said, "There go that fool right there!" Big Tim started walking faster.

"I caught up to him, and told him there was no way that O'Shea was the somebody we needed to check. He ignored me and pulled out the stick. I got in front of him and tried to stop him. He hit me in my junk with the stick, and I fell. When I got up it was too late."

Mike dropped his head. He paused for a few seconds and then went on, "O'Shea looked at Big Tim and then at me. Then I heard, "Pop! Pop!" Big Tim hit him twice in the stomach. O'Shea didn't even see it coming. It was like Big Tim ignored Hank's orders. He didn't give O'Shea a warning or anything. He just shot!"

D.L. stopped pacing the floor at Mike's conclusion. He stood in the middle of the living room with his arms crossed, his lips buttoned, and a scowl on his face.

"Say something, D.L.!"

"First of all," said D.L. "I found out about you working for Hank. And secondly, you were set up!"

"What?!" Mike stood up. "How you figure?"

"Let's talk about it in the morning. The police are probably looking for you right now." D.L. walked Mike to the door. "You got a place to stay tonight?"

"I got a place in mind."

"Good. We'll meet up early. Answer your phone when I call."

* * *

D.L. fought his way through the tail-end of the morning rush and walked straight to the information desk at the hospital. As he neared the room O'Shea was in, he noticed a detective standing outside the room talking on his phone. D.L. slowed his approach in hopes that the detective would reveal some new information about O'Shea's shooting. D.L. quickened his pace after he heard the detective say to the person on the other end of the phone, "I haven't questioned him yet. He's still sedated."

D.L. reached for the door lever to enter O'Shea's room, but he was denied by the nurse who suddenly appeared. After a brief explanation, she escorted D.L. to the waiting room where O'Shea's mother, Ms. Tate, was sitting. D.L. embraced Ms. Tate with a long hug. He sat down next to her and held her hand as she told him about the horrible phone call she got late in the night. D.L. wondered if her phone rang at the exact moment Mike knocked on his apartment door.

When Ms. Tate's conversation switched to O'Shea and D.L. as younger boys, D.L.'s thoughts also started to shift. She began talking about the foot races the neighborhood boys used to have, and D.L. thought about the empty chairs in the waiting room. D.L. counted a dozen empty chairs, and for each chair he named a person O'Shea helped or tried to help.

D.L. looked up at the ceiling and thought, "O'Shea made a big impact on so many people, yet the only one in his corner is his mama." As if she could hear what D.L. was thinking, Ms. Tate started to weep. D.L. gave her hand a squeeze. They sat in silence.

They were escorted to O'Shea's room and paused along his bedside. O'Shea was connected to several machines in his uncomfortable slumber. D.L. took a mental picture of his friend, and then he reached in his pocket and pulled out a handful of O'Shea's favorite candy. D.L. put the candy on the side table and gave Ms. Tate a farewell hug. He patted O'Shea on the shoulder, then left the hospital.

From the hospital, D.L. drove to an unfamiliar apartment building and parked in the back of it. He took a hard look around at his surroundings and then he waited. Mike walked out five minutes later. He had on an extra-large emerald green sweatshirt with a matching snapback. Mike hopped in the car and D.L. drove off.

At the first red light, D.L. looked over at Mike and asked, "One quick question, bruh?"

"Sup?"

D.L. tried hard not to laugh. "Is it just me, or are you aiming for that jolly green giant look? Ho, ho, ho!" He cracked up.

"Your laughter is inappropriate, Darius," fussed Mike in a sarcastic tone. Then he changed the subject, "How about a hot buttered biscuit for your baby brother? I'm hungry."

D.L. ignored him. They traveled through several street-lights without the exchange of words. Mike took off his snapback and the oversized sweatshirt. He leaned back in his seat and covered his face with his hands. Then he peeped over at D.L. "You think I was set up?"

"Consider this. You were put on a different type of mission with unclear information. And it was your boy Big Tim who attacked O'Shea, out of all people. Big Tim even pushed you off when you tried to stop him. It all sounds funny to me, bruh. I think it's pretty obvious that Hank set you up."

"But why would Hank set me up?" Mike stalled, "He's, my brother."

D.L. took in a deep breath then slowly let it out. "Maybe he's trying to get back at me for paying him a visit yesterday. I told him that you weren't his puppet anymore."

All in the same motion, Mike sat up and punched the dash-board, "I got it! It wasn't Hank at all!"

"How do you know?"

"It was all Big Tim!"

"Are you sure?" D.L. wondered.

"About two weeks ago, Tim told me he was going to stop working for Hank and run with this dude named Freddy. He asked if I was in. I told him no and didn't think anything else about it. I guess he wanted to take both me and O'Shea out. He wanted to take O'Shea out, so that he wouldn't get in his business, and he wants me gone for staying loyal to Hank. Yep, he's gonna try to pen this on me!"

"And that's why we gotta clear your name," D.L. interrupted. You got a big fight in front of you little bruh, but we warriors so you'll get through this."

D.L. slid through the driveway of a local breakfast shop. Once he received the food, he parked in a distant spot. Mike unwrapped the first biscuit and went to work on it.

With one bite left, he paused long enough to admit, "I don't think I can do it, D.L."

D.L. took a sip from his coffee, "Do what?"

Mike took a long pull of orange juice from his straw. "If it comes down to it, I don't think I'll be able to snitch on Big Tim."

"What did you say, Mikey?"

"Look! I know you want me to turn myself in, but I can't snitch."

D.L. rammed his fist against the steering wheel a couple times, and then he took a deep breath before starting a conversation with himself, "I don't get it. We got the same mama, but I got all the smarts and this one here has misguided loyalties and the intelligence of a rock."

D.L. then directed the argument toward Mike, "First of all, the word snitch doesn't even apply here. That's O'Shea in the ICU hanging on to dear life. The same O'Shea that used to give you money for candy when the boys at the bus stop used to take coins from your crybaby behind! The same O'Shea that made Boogie return your bike when he stole it from your hollering butt!

D.L. nudged Mike's arm with his elbow, "He's the same O'Shea, Mikey, that's in your face and everybody else's face, asking you to change. Not in a disrespectful way, but in a way that makes you wanna check yourself."

Mike balled up the paper from his second biscuit and put it in the trash bag on the floor. He spoke softly at first, "I get it."

"I didn't hear you. Can you say it again?" asked D.L.

"I said I get it, and I got it! Now let's go!"

* * *

After passing through the metal detectors at the police station, D.L. and Mike paused to observe the busy flow of people moving to and from. Mike spotted an officer directing people from a small kiosk. They approached the officer, and D.L. explained that they were there to talk to someone about a serious crime. The officer pointed them in the direction of the criminal investigation's unit.

They entered a less crowded area of the police station, mostly occupied by detectives. D.L. walked up to the first desk he saw and repeated the mission. They were invited to sit down in a make-do waiting room. They sat in fold up chairs that were neatly placed along a side wall. Their view consisted of a massive house plant, a water cooler, a giant picture of the mayor, and a small elevator.

A door from one of the interrogation rooms swung open. Two officers walked out and escorted a handcuffed man to the elevator. The handcuffed man was short and stocky, and he wore dark skinny jeans, a black sweatshirt and a Raiders hat. When the doors opened, the man was escorted in by the two officers. The stocky man slowly turned around then locked eyes with Mike. He gave a cheesy grin and a quick wink. When the doors closed, D.L. and Mike looked at each other. The man in the elevator was Big Tim.

Mike was called into the interrogation room alone. At Mike's request, D.L. joined him an hour later. The detective pulled out a chair for D.L. and stood in the middle of the room. Mike sat quietly in the corner, handcuffed and angrier than a starving lion. D.L. turned to the detective for answers, "So what's the situation?"

"I just formally charged your brother with attempted murder," announced Detective Morris. "I'm waiting on an escort team to take him down to processing."

"You got the wrong person, detective. My brother didn't shoot O'Shea!"

"So, you were there too?" quizzed the detective in a smug voice.

"No, I wasn't. But Mike didn't shoot O'Shea. O'Shea is like family to us."

The detective interrupted D.L. "Save your gummy bear stories about how close you are to O'Shea." His voice grew impatient. "I heard it all before! In fact, Timothy told me the exact same thing, only he told me before your brother did!"

Detective Morris moved closer to D.L. "The problem is that neither one is taking the blame for pulling the trigger, but they both admitted to being there when it happened. So, I have no choice but to charge them both."

"What happens next?" asked D.L.

"We're going to keep investigating. If your brother is telling the truth, I suggest you get him a good attorney for his day in court. But there is one more thing."

"And what's that?"

The detective looked at Mike while stating his last point, "O'Shea is a good man. Pray that he pulls through."

There was a knock on the door. D.L. stood to his feet and then he helped Mike out of his chair. D.L. watched as Mike stepped into the half-sized elevator with two uniformed officers at his side. Once the doors closed, D.L. turned in the opposite direction and left the police station half dazed.

* * *

D.L. called his mother to convince her to leave work early. He picked up lunch from the drive-through window of The Burger Joint, and met her at the apartment around 1:30 that afternoon. Ms. Jeffries's face was painted with stress. She lit up a cigarette then she asked, "Is my baby dead?"

"What? Mama, no! This is no way to live! What makes you think Mikey is dead?"

She took a long pull from her cigarette and started pacing. "I ain't seen him since earlier yesterday. After he left, you came by telling me he's in trouble. And now we meet up in the middle of the day when we're both supposed to be at work." She looked up at D.L. with long sad eyes. "What am I supposed to think?"

D.L. flopped down on the couch the same way he did so many times before. He looked at his mother and blurted, "Mikey got arrested."

Ms. Jeffries stopped pacing and sat down next to D.L. She put the cigarette out in the ashtray and kicked it across the room. With irritation in her voice, she took a deep breath and then asked, "What did he do?"

D.L. began the story from the moment Mike knocked on his door in the middle of the night. He shared every detail about the day before and ended the story at the moment the elevator doors closed Mike in. Ms. Jeffries cried hard at the news that O'Shea was heartlessly gunned down. She shed extra tears knowing that her youngest son was involved.

Moments later, Ms. Jeffries dabbed away her tears. She opened the window and then she retrieved her laptop from the bedroom. D.L. grabbed the burgers from the bag and gave one to his mother. Over slightly warm hamburgers and the sound of the quiet streets, they conducted their search for a really good lawyer.

* * *

Mike was escorted from his cell to the visitation center across campus. Once inside the private room, his handcuffs and shackles were removed and he was free to move around. The officer left Mike in the company of D.L. and their mother.

Mike kissed his mother on the cheek and pulled out a chair directly across from her.

D.L. examined Mike's orange jump suit and teased, "I thought green was your color?"

Mike snapped. "Don't nobody feel like joking, D.L. You got some news for me? If not, I might as well go back to my cell!"

Ms. Jeffries smacked D.L. on the back of his head and scolded him, "That wasn't cool!" She then turned to Mike. "What's up with the attitude? I thought you would be happy to see us."

"Ain't nothing happy about this place, Mama!" Mike took in a deep breath then changed his previous tone, "Mama, I'm not going to be happy until I leave here. Anybody got news about my case?"

Ms. Jeffries answered, "We found you a really good lawyer, and your court date is in two weeks."

"Two weeks!"

D.L. spoke up, "Quit crying Mikey. It could be much worse."

"Whateva, man! How is O'Shea?"

"It ain't looking too good. I went to check on him a couple days ago. Mama Tate said he came around and was even talking a bit. She couldn't make out most of what he was saying, but it was progress." D.L. paused long enough to let out a long slow breath, "He slipped back into a coma after that."

Mike stood to his feet. "I need y'all to understand something before you leave here today. I did not shoot O'Shea, and I didn't know what Big Tim was up to. Had I known, I would've done anything to stop him. And I mean anything!" Heavy tears started to fall off the bottom of his face.

"Sit down Mikey," pleaded Ms. Jefferies. She dug in her purse for tissue. "I know you didn't hurt O'Shea. I didn't raise you to be heartless."

She handed him a small pack of tissue.

"You've done some dumb things in the past," added D.L. "But this ain't you, and anybody who knows you would say the same thing."

"None of that matters, D.L.! So, I guess I'm at the mercy of the court, huh?" Mike started pacing back and forth.

"I'm working on something that might shed light on your case," revealed D.L. "I should have some more info before the court date."

Mike stopped pacing when the officer knocked on the window and signaled that he had five minutes of visitation time left.

"The word of the day is hope. You gotta keep hope in your heart, son," assured Ms. Jeffries. She stood up and gave Mike a long hug. She placed a hand on his chest and continued, "Without it, there is only doom."

Ms. Jeffries ended their visit with a short prayer. Mike's wrists were handcuffed in front of his body and a plastic band was tied around his ankles. He was escorted back down the long hallway and across campus to his cell.

D.L. quickly ate up the miles on the return trip, and Ms. Jeffries was not shy about expressing her concern, "Why are you driving so fast, boy?!"

"I told you, Mama. I gotta handle something. I'm trying to help Mike."

When he pulled to the curb, it took Ms. Jefferies a while to open the car door. "I'm sorry it's taking me so long," she teased, "I would've been in the house already if I didn't have whiplash!"

"Mama, you a whole mess," he joked, "now get out of my car!" He waited until she was out of view, and he then peeled off.

D.L. drove around the perimeter of the gas station where O'Shea had been shot. He closely examined the building and gave extra consideration to the corners of the tattered building. Finally, he parked his car, scratched the back of his head, and then entered the gas station. He merged into the single line of customers. There were two people in front of him and another person behind him. When he approached the counter, he asked to talk to the owner of the gas station, but the attendant gave him a hard time.

"Are you the owner or not?"

"You buy gas or you buy items," the attendant responded. "I don't understand anything else."

D.L. was not the only one growing impatient. The boy behind him in line huffed and puffed. D.L. stood to the side and allowed the boy to check out. D.L. took a step closer to the attendant. "I need to talk to the owner of this gas station."

"The owner is not in the country," he responded. "I'm the closest thing you got."

"What happened to the surveillance cameras that were in-stalled outside this building?"

"Surveillance cameras? There were never any surveillance cameras. We're barely making even; I can't afford surveillance cameras!"

"I have reason to believe that you aren't being honest. Are you going to let me see the tapes or not?"

The attendant swiftly changed back to an annoying mono-tone, "You buy gas, you buy items, or you leave."

D.L. left and sought out Detective Morris, the officer in charge of investigating the case. He arranged for the detective to meet him outside the police station. D.L. found a parking spot in front of the building and waited. Detective Morris opened the door right away and hopped in the passenger's seat.

"So D.L., shouldn't you be working on child welfare crimes and leaving us to do our job?"

"That's funny detective. I see you did your homework on me."

"Well, I had ten minutes to kill before you arrived. So, you got a tip for me about your brother's case?"

"I was talking to O'Shea the same day he got shot. He men-tioned something about the gas station being a hot spot for crime. I could've sworn he said that he persuaded the owner to install security cameras. I just spoke to the manager, and he said they never had any cameras. But O'Shea's word is like good glue. You know?"

"That's interesting," the detective replied as he got out the car. "Thanks for the tip, D.L. And the next time you get a hunch, hand it over to me, and I'll take it from there. Don't go asking questions anymore. That could ruin things." Detective Morris closed D.L.'s car door then disappeared into the building.

* * *

Instead of taking the highway, D.L. took the scenic route back to his apartment. He was less than a mile away from his door when the text message alert popped on his phone. He switched over to the slow lane and decreased his speed just in time to catch the red light. The message was from O'Shea's nurse, Ta'Niya. It read, "*He took a turn for the worse. Get here when you can.*"

D.L. made the necessary route changes that led him to the freeway and back in the direction of downtown. He parked in the garage closest to the elevators. He walked into the hospital and right past the information desk. D.L. stepped out the elevator and turned toward O'Shea's room.

Detective Morris stood in the hallway directly across from O'Shea's room. His phone was pressed firmly against his ear. With the same impact of a flying brick, the words hit D.L. in his chest, when the detective spoke into his phone, "This is now a homicide case." He ended the call and put his phone back in his pocket. He saw D.L. approaching and began walking toward him to get to the elevators. "Miserable news ahead," he declared as he darted past D.L. He did not break pace.

The door to O'Shea's room opened and nurse Ta'Niya came out. She gently pushed D.L. away from the door and looked up at him, "You made it here quickly, and that's a good thing. But it's bad in there. That poor woman."

"How long since he passed?"

She reached into her scrubs and pulled out her phone, "Almost an hour ago." She gave him a pat on the arm and moved out the way. "Be strong in there."

O'Shea was surrounded by his mother and two aunts. One of his aunts stood in the corner crying uncontrollably. Ms. Tate stood on O'Shea's left, and the other aunt stood on his right. They were both patting his wide shoulders and begging him to wake up. D.L. stood frozen in a soundtrack of soul-ripping moans. He was lost in a whirlwind of emotions and unable to speak. Nurse Ta'Niya walked in the room a few minutes later with two orderlies. "It's time, Ms. Tate," announced Ta'Niya. The orderlies rolled O'shea's body away.

* * *

D.L. parked in front of the funeral home and looked around. Unlike the waiting room at the hospital, people showed up at O'Shea's wake. D.L. saw people he had not seen in years. There were deacons, street hustlers, school kids, ex-convicts, little old church ladies, drug dealers, and teachers. Almost everyone wore a t-shirt with O'Shea's picture on it.

D.L. tried to exit his car, but he could not. He set there instead with his hand on the door. He was content with watching the people come and go while pondering over old memories of his good friend. A short time later, D.L met eyes with an older lady leaving the funeral home. He stared at her until he recognized her face. It was the same lady in the flower printed dress that he stood next to at the crime scene in his old neighborhood. D.L. started the car and left.

D.L. stayed busy in his office the following day, until he received a text from his mother. It was time for O'Shea's funeral. D.L. picked her up then drove to the church across the street from the funeral home. He parked in the same parking spot from the day before. Ms. Jeffries turned toward him and placed a kind hand on his arm, "I saw you sitting in your car yesterday when I left the wake. Did you ever make it inside?"

"I almost did, Mama."

"Will you be joining me for the funeral today?"

D.L. shook his head no.

"I figured as much, but I had to ask."

He got out and walked around to open the door for his mother. He helped her out the car and gave her a hug. Then he leaned up against his car and looked up into the heavens.

As a child, D.L. was forced to sit through the funeral services of deceased family members. He bore the pain of the souls who understood life and the misguided pain of those who did not. He endured the walk toward the casket and the observation of the barely recognizable flesh of the dead. He tolerated the odd smell of the embalmed body, the testimonies of personal accounts, and the sermons on how to feel. He suffered through the sad songs that encouraged weeping. D.L. hated funeral, and now that he was old enough to make the call, he endured them no more.

D.L. got back in his car and reclined in his seat. He imagined O'Shea dressed in a white suit relaxing at a royal dinner table. With his hands folded behind his head, O'Shea boasted a wonderful smile. He stood up from the table and rubbed his belly in total satisfaction. He walked on clouds until he spotted an apple tree through the clearing. He picked an apple from the tree and then rested his long frame against the tree's trunk. As he bit into the apple, O'Shea began to speak to the angels that surrounded him. They were delighted with his message, and he was just as pleased to be delivering it. His words were unconceivable to D.L., but he could almost hear the tone of O'Shea's voice. And just as quickly as it came, the vision disappeared from D.L.'s mind.

Ms. Jeffries returned to the car with a tag for the windshield. D.L. followed the long line of cars to the cemetery. He joined his mother and all the others in a final fare-well to O'Shea at the grave site. D.L. inhaled the fresh air and welcomed the gentle breeze. The Pastor said a closing prayer and the casket was slowly deposited into the earth. D.L. peered into the hole and tossed in a rose. He embraced Ms. Tate with a long hug and then left the cemetery with his mother.

* * *

D.L. had just completed a home-visit on the same side of town as the juvenile correctional facility. He paid Mike a visit. D.L found a parking spot, went through the necessary screenings to enter the facility, then waited for his brother in the small visiting room. While waiting, D.L. thought about Mike's disastrous day in court a week earlier.

With his lawyer by his side, Mike entered the court room right before the judge walked in. Mike looked like a helpless ten-year old in a state issued jumpsuit. The judge was efficient and she required quick and precise answers. The prosecutor answered first with a small list of charges with first-degree murder as the highlight. Mike's lawyer pleaded not guilty on his behalf and Mike was returned to custody. The whole ordeal lasted no more than 10 minutes. It left D.L. and Ms. Jeffries with three key phrases to ponder for Mike's future trail: tried as an adult, maximum security prison, and life without parole.

Mike dragged into the visiting room and hung out next to the door, "Did Mama send you up here?"

"Nope. Sit down, Mikey."

Mike hesitated. "You haven't been here in like two weeks. Why today? It ain't my birthday."

"I wanted to give you space after that day in court."

"O' yeah. Court. Wasn't that beautiful?" Mike laughed. "But you know what's even more beautiful?"

D.L.'s head fell into his chest, "What's that, Mikey?"

"The light that you shed on my case." He laughed again, "That was awesome. What an assist, bruh!"

D.L. lifted his head, "I thought I had my hands on a tape that captured what happened that night at the gas station, but it didn't work out."

"That sums up my life, don't it, bruh?" He repeated D.L.'s words, "It didn't work out." Mike stood to his feet, "Well, it's been real, D.L. I'll see you at my sentencing or some random day at the penitentiary if you decide to drop by."

"Sit down, Mikey, and quit acting like you're two!"

Mike ignored him and started pounding on the door. "You sound just like Mama, D.L. What's the word of the day, hope? Nah, that was two weeks ago. Let's see," he scratched the top of his head. "What about trust? Nope, that was last week." Mike paused long enough for the guard to enter the room and put the handcuffs back on him.

"I got it, bruh! The word of the day is... it didn't work out!"

Mike was led out the room, but D.L. had the last words, "Keep the faith, Mikey!"

THREE MONTHS LATER

D.L. had just walked out of court with one of his clients when he felt his phone vibrate. He bid a final farewell to his client whose case had finally been closed after three long years. D.L. took off his suit coat and snapped loose the top button on his polo. He responded to his mother's text and then he put on his shades and stepped into the sunshine.

He pulled up to his mother's apartment building and blew the horn to announce his arrival. He called his secretary to let her know that he would not be returning to the office. Ms. Jeffries strapped herself into the passenger's seat, and D.L. drove toward the freeway. At the first stoplight he formally greeted her with a kiss to the cheek, "You look pretty. And you look nervous. You alright, mama?"

Looking straight ahead and without a blink she answered, "I'll be fine."

"You sure, Mama? We could go get something to eat and do a little shopping instead. Then I can drop you off and go get ready for my date with Ta'Niya tonight."

The light turned green, but D.L. paused with his foot still on the brake. With a half-smile on his face, he turned toward his mother and waited for her response.

She let out a quick laugh and then answered, "Keep driving, Darius. You a mess!"

"As you wish, mama. Just remember that I tried to give you an out."

He came to a stop in front of the juvenile correctional facility. The moment his mother got out the car, he started the search for a parking spot along the street. He eventually found a space to back into, then he locked the doors, reclined, and adjusted the mirrors to his satisfaction. D.L. closed his eyes and allowed his working memory within to map out the events that led him to that exact parking spot.

His memory took him back to the day he ran into nurse Ta'Niya outside the hospital. She was taking a smoke break. He had just finished visiting a hospitalized client. With an empty coffee cup dancing around in his hand, D.L. lectured Ta'Niya on the effects of nicotine. In return, she made him aware of the effects of excessive caffeine drinking. By the end of their conversation, a date had been planned where the two of them would meet up for dinner with O'Shea's mother, Ms. Tate.

D.L. and Ta'Niya met up at Ms. Tate's home that Friday evening. The three of them feasted on Ta'Niya's creation of mushroom chicken and angel hair pasta and sipped on Ms.

Tate's home brewed iced tea. Ms. Tate shared her super thick photo album with them and talked about O'Shea as a child. D.L. apologized to Ms. Tate on behalf of his family and assured her that Mike was not responsible for what happened to O'Shea. D.L. then served up his contribution, store-bought chocolate cupcakes with white icing.

Ms. Tate escorted them to the door after dinner, but before she opened it, she paused. She revealed to D.L. that while in the hospital, O'Shea was talking gibberish about a tape. She paused again to gather her thoughts.

Her concentration was deep. "He was talking slowly and it didn't make any sense to me, but he said it real loud like it was important. He said, *I was testing the camera.* What camera, baby? I asked him. And then he said, *Give the tape to D.L. or the detective.* What tape, baby? I asked him. All he said after that was, *smooth.* He was too tired to say anything else. That probably don't mean nothing to nobody, D.L., but it was on my heart to tell you."

When D.L. made it home that night, he sat in his recliner. He pondered over the fact that there was an important tape somewhere that O'Shea wanted him or the detective to have. In addition to the whereabouts of the tape, D.L. started to obsess over the word *smooth.* He stood to his feet when he found a connection. He picked up his phone and called Detective Morris.

D.L. met the detective that night at his favorite coffee shop downtown. D.L. told him about the story that Ms. Tate shared with him. He also told the detective about a former neighborhood guardian named Smooth who use to stay across the street from the gas station where O'Shea was shot. Detective Morris accepted D.L.'s intel and told him to expect a follow-up call in a few days.

D.L. parked outside the apartment building that was across the street from the gas station. It was 8:00 A.M. on a Saturday. He took sips from his coffee and took in the surroundings. D.L. estimated that the old brick building contained eighteen apartment units. He spotted an apartment on the second floor. The bright yellow curtains and hanging garden bed caused it to stand out. D.L.'s eyes followed that apartment to the one above it. He rubbed his eyes and then squinted to get a better view. Attached to the outside of that apartment was a small surveillance camera, and the barely visible camera pointed directly at the gas station.

Detective Morris tapped on D.L.'s window and diverted his attention. D.L. eased his window down.

"What are you doing here, D.L.?"

"Same thing you are."

"I told you to expect my call in a few days."

"Let's just say I'm eager." He pointed up at the small camera.

"You gotta know that you can't be here while I'm questioning this man," said the detective. He smacked the top of D.L.'s car in frustration.

D.L. rolled his window back up and got out the car. He looked the detective in his face, "I was here first. Besides, I'm just visiting an old friend. You can join me if you like."

D.L. took off toward the building and the detective hesitantly followed.

They climbed the stairs up to the third floor and paused outside the apartment. "Leave the questions to me," declared Detective Morris.

They took turns knocking on the door. Smooth eventually answered and let them in. D.L. and Detective Morris followed his tall frame and the smell of hard liquor to the living room. They sat down on the couch after he pointed it out to them.

Smooth's apartment was small and to the point. There was a couch, a recliner, and a coffee table. There was also an old projection TV on a wooden stand and a bookshelf in the corner. It was lined with framed certificates and dusty basketball trophies.

D.L. reflected back to his days in elementary school when Smooth was a ghetto super star. He was the best high-school basketball player in the city and all the boys tried to mimic his style at recess. D.L. thought back to the time he ran into Smooth after his ball playing years were over. The coach at the neighborhood center stopped the games and made all the boys listen to a speech given by Smooth. After hearing him speak, D.L. felt guilty about teaching Mike how to represent for the neighborhood set. Before he could make things right, Mike got brutally jumped a few days later.

Smooth sat in his recliner after D.L. and the detective took their seats. He turned up the bottle that was in his hand and added it to the collection of empty bottles on the coffee table. "Who are y'all and what do y'all want?"

Detective Morris introduced himself and explained his order of business, but Smooth fell asleep midway through the detective's opening statement. The detective pulled out a fifth of brown liquor and slammed it on the coffee table. Smooth popped up and reached for the bottle.

"You gotta answer my questions first," the detective teased. He placed the bottle out of Smooth's reach.

"Who are y'all?" snapped Smooth a second time. "And let me get a swallow of that."

"I'm detective Morris, and I got a few questions about your friend, O'Shea. Help me out and the bottle is yours."

"O'Shea was a good dude! He cared about this neighborhood, man. He could have left, but he didn't."

"Did he say anything about setting up a camera to keep tabs on the activity at the gas station across the street?"

"O'Shea was always talking about ways to better this hood, man. He reminded me of myself back in the day. He might've said something along that note, but what do I know? I'm passed out half the time." He clapped his hands together in anticipation, "Now pass me that drink."

The detective ignored his request, "So you don't know anything about the camera outside your window?"

Smooth scooted to the edge of the chair. His eyes were bloodshot red and bucked, "Camera? Outside my window? You sure about that?"

All three of them stood up. D.L. and the detective followed Smooth into his kitchen. It was a challenge, but he managed to open the window above the sink. He stuck his head out then responded, "How in the world?"

D.L. stuck his arm out the window, retrieved the camera, and gave it to Detective Morris. He took a deep breath then pressed the eject button. When the memory card popped out, he held it up to show D.L., "Here goes your tape." The detective gave Smooth the bottle, and they hurried out the building. They met up at the police station.

Detective Morris's workspace was small but neat. Every trinket was in place and the family photos provided a welcoming balance to an otherwise hard-nosed work environment. Detective Morris pushed in the memory card, and they hovered over his computer screen.

He clicked on the first file and O'Shea came alive. He was in Smooth's living room giving an introduction. "Hey y'all, this me!" He was loud and cheerful. "I'm testing out my new IP camera. This my baby!" He looked directly into the lens of the camera and gave a big smile. "You see that gas station across the street?" He put the camera to the window and zoomed in. "Things get real ugly over there, but let's see if your boy can fix that."

He turned the camera back on himself, "I'm about to put my baby in place. Then I'm going over there to see how she works." The clip stopped and the computer screen went blank.

The second clip showed a close up of the gas station. There was a truck parked out front. O'Shea walked into the gas station minutes later. When he walked out, he stood outside the entrance and waved at the camera. A guy on a bike rolled up to O'Shea and started talking to him. Another person from inside the gas station walked out and joined the conversation. They talked for a while, and then the guy on the bike peddled off. The other guy got in his truck and drove off a few seconds later.

As the truck left the parking lot, the camera picked up two people walking toward the gas station. It was Big Tim and Mike. They were stride for stride at first, but Big Tim pulled something out of his pants and started walking faster. Mike caught up to Big Tim and shoved him in the chest. They tussled for a few seconds then Big Tim pushed Mike to the ground. Big Tim stepped over Mike then continued his approached. Big Tim took aim at O'Shea and shot him from ten feet away. Detective Morris clicked the stop button.

D.L.'s eyes popped open the moment he heard Mike yell his name. D.L. got out the car and greeted Mike with a hug. D.L. and Ms. Jeffries were forced to listen to Mike's jailhouse stories and his I-can't-wait-to speeches. At the stoplight, D.L. looked over at his mother and taunted, "It's too late now, but you should've taken the out."

Ms. Jeffries rolled her eyes and replied, "Don't I know it?"

D.L. dropped their mother off at home and Mike hopped into the passenger's seat. D.L. drove to the cemetery and parked outside the gate. D.L. traced his memory back to O'Shea's grave site and Mike followed. A welcoming wind directed their separate yet silent conversations with O'Shea. Lingering song birds kept a respectful distance.

On the slow walk back to the car, D.L. challenged Mike with a question, "So what's next, bruh?"

"I'm going back to school, and I'm going to finish. And then after that, I'm not too sure."

"What did you and O'Shea talk about the last time you spoke to him?"

"He was talking to me about legacy. I heard him, but I wasn't really listening. His words came back to me while I was waiting for the judge to send me to the pen. I was thinking, what if by some miracle I was let out of jail and got to start all over again? What would I do? Hustling is easy green, and I'm really good at it, bruh. But then what? Back to jail? Erased from this earth? Nah. I'm hoping it's a lot more to life." He looked up at D.L. and said, "I'm for real."

"Wow," replied D.L. "That was beautiful."

"For the first time in a long time, I'm serious, Darius."

"I feel you, Mikey. And whatever you decide, you got my support."

"Cool!" They got back in the car. Mike put on his seatbelt then asked, "How about a butter bacon burger for your baby brother?"

D.L.'s comeback was quick, "How about a fried salami sandwich with cheese and mustard from your mama's kitchen?"

"You know what?" Mike laughed, "That sounds delicious!"

THE END